THE FAIREST HEART

HEATHER CHAPMAN

Front cover design by Amanda Conley

Edited by Jolene Perry

Printed by Heather Chapman, in the United States of America.

First printing edition 2019.

http://www.heatherchapmanauthor.com

For a complete list of Heather Chapman's books or to sign up for her newsletter, visit http://www.heatherchapmanauthor.com

For Charlotte, Ruby, and Ivy
There is nothing more beautiful than kindness.

CHAPTER 1

Hampshire Countryside, England
May, 1814

Memories were curious things, one moment slicing through one's reverie—often at the least expected times—then evading one in a moment of need. Rose Grant had often wished she could command such recollections, summoning the pleasant and banishing the sorrowful. But life hadn't played out to be so simple, nor so neat. Memories had a will of their own and showed themselves at the least convenient times.

She brushed her fingers across the stone ledge of the well where she sat. Her heart teetered, half in pain, half in pleasure. The memory of her mother had come so suddenly, without the slightest of warning. An aching pulsed in her chest, and Rose took in a deep breath.

Her mother's features came to mind once more. Rose attempted to memorize her mother's smile, the way her teeth aligned against her full and crimson lips, the slant of her darkened eyes, and the dark lashes that held a cheery curl.

A single tear slipped down her cheek. The picture was

already fading, slipping into fogginess and forced imaginings. Rose sighed and looked down the dark hole below.

Twelve years prior, Rose had sat in that exact spot and watched with wonder as her mother had dropped the bucket into the well. *"This might as well be a wishing well,"* her mother had said, eyes widening when the bucket made a splash at the bottom. *"For no matter how many times I drop the bucket, there is always water to be found."*

The act had seemed magical at the time, as if Rose's mother had conjured something out of nothing, and Rose had often leaned against the stone walls of the well to watch as servants collected water. Years of watching and wishing, and only rarely did the memory come in its purest form.

Horse hooves clipped against the gravel drive, crashing into Rose's thoughts. She flinched at the sound but did not rise to survey the guest. The footman would undoubtedly be waiting on the bottom steps of Grant Estate, ever at the ready to assist the guest into the parlor where Aunt Prudence would be waiting.

The well, situated among the kitchen garden, was a much more suitable place for Rose. She was curious—yes. Guests seemed to flock to Grant Estate more days than not, and Aunt Prudence entertained the most fashionable, reputable ladies of Hampshire—some guests traveling from as far as London. Though, Rose often wondered whether those guests came to visit her aunt or Grant Estate.

While Aunt Prudence was well known to be an established beauty, she paled in comparison with the country charm of Rose's childhood home. The house itself was built in the Queen Anne style. Red and blue brick, set in English bond, covered the front of the house. The three levels boasted eight family bedrooms, a reception hall, two drawing rooms, a cozy breakfast nook, a dining hall that could seat up to twenty guests, a sizable library, a snug study, and—perhaps Rose's favorite—a comfortable room for dancing.

If ever there was a perfectly situated estate, Rose believed it to be Grant Estate. For more than the charming architecture and impeccably well-kept condition, the wild beauty of the gardens and countryside stretched as far as the eye could see. Spring was especially delightful.

"Miss Grant."

Rose startled, rising in an instant.

The butler stood at the arched doorway. His bushy brows were tangled together in a customary scowl, and his oversized mouth rested in a frown. "Your aunt requests you join her in the drawing room," he said, dipping his chin.

"Thank you, Mr. Browning. If you could be so kind as to inform her I am on my way. I have only to put my flowers in water." Rose bent to retrieve the basket at her feet.

The dog-roses in the field adjacent to the stables had been too exquisite to pass by on her morning walk. The light pink flowers were a cheerful distraction from the heaviness in the house beyond the butler.

Mr. Browning cleared his throat. "If you will allow me, I will take the flowers to the housekeeper to arrange."

Rose hesitated. She had spent the better part of her entire life with Mr. Browning as butler, but she hardly knew him. She handed him the flowers with reluctance. "I shall join my aunt as you suggest. Please have the flowers sent to my bedchamber. Thank you."

He dipped into a bow. "As you wish, Miss Grant."

Aunt Prudence rarely requested the presence of Rose, and if she did, it was invariably to scold her niece. Rose ran a hand over her chignon. Loose curls escaped, and she sighed. Working in the garden, however therapeutic, would be sure to earn a bold chastisement. Such things always did.

At times, Rose believed her aunt to rather enjoy humiliating her. There was something about the way Aunt Prudence's nose pinched and her lips curled into a sardonic smirk that hinted at the possibility—not to mention the way her aunt's voice lifted in excitement whenever she relayed one of Rose's unfortunate happenings. Rose shivered; such thoughts were unkind. Allowances were to be made for such people as Prudence.

Her aunt, as handsome as she was, was single and nearing six and forty. Her life had been filled with caring for another's child, and not just any child—the daughter of a much-preferred brother.

Rose passed through the kitchen, trying her best to avoid the notice of the cook. Mrs. Blackburn was already preparing midday tea, busied about the stove and cakes on the nearby table.

"Out in the gardens again, Miss Grant?" Mrs. Blackburn said, turning. Her light eyes seemed to twinkle, but then her lips fell into a frown. "Your aunt has expressly forbidden you from venturing outdoors without a bonnet, and where are your gloves?"

Rose studied the tiles beneath her feet. The coolness of the stones seeped through her slippers, sending a shiver up her spine. She hung her head. "Please do not tell her, Mrs. Blackburn. The day was lovely, and the sun was not so hot as to require a bonnet."

The cook placed a heavy hand against her hip and let out a raspy complaint. "I quite agree, but you know how your aunt carries on. She'll only continue making your life more difficult if you do not comply."

"I know," Rose said, shaking her head. She had likened Aunt Prudence's presence to a dark cloud, looming over Grant Estate, too many times to count. Her aunt was unbearably strict and stern and disapproving of everyone—and nearly everything. "I will try to be better."

"Do," Mrs. Blackburn said before turning back to her cakes. "And I shall forget I saw you."

A smile snuck across Rose's cheeks. Despite her aunt's role as appointed lady of the house—and her constant efforts to appear so—Mrs. Blackburn and most of the other servants still regarded Rose with more consideration. "Thank you."

Rose scurried down the hall, pausing to stop in the foyer. She fanned her cheeks and steadied her scattered breaths, before inching toward the open door to the east drawing room. Muffled voices and laughter drifted to her ears. Another step revealed three guests, seated at the side of her aunt—Mrs. Lockhart and her two daughters.

Rose exhaled in relief. They were some of Rose's oldest acquaintances, and Mrs. Lockhart had been particularly close to Rose's mother.

"Goodness, no. My niece would do just as well to stay home with her grandfather... No, I'm quite certain. She would not wish the company, sad girl that she is." Aunt Prudence let out a nasally giggle. "She hardly speaks to anyone besides her grandfather and the horses."

Uneasiness nearly choked Rose, but she tapped against the open door to announce her presence. "Aunt," she said, offering a low curtsy. "Mr. Browning said you requested to see me."

Aunt Prudence's eyes narrowed. "And not even a greeting to our guests, my my."

Rose winced. "Forgive me. Good day, Mrs. Lockhart. Good day, Miss Lockhart and Miss Mary. I do hope you are well."

Mrs. Lockhart stood, followed by her daughters. She took Rose's hands in her own. "Dear Rose, I was hoping you would join us on an afternoon walk. The flowers are so lovely this time of year and none lovelier than here."

Excitement flickered across Rose's face. Months had

passed since she had visited with the Lockhart family. "I would be glad—"

"Not at all," Aunt Prudence interrupted. "I'm afraid Rose is indisposed this afternoon. I have only called her here to remind her that her grandfather has not been attended to. My father does so like his readings every day."

"But he would not mind if I were to postpone our reading an hour." Rose knew Mrs. Lockhart would appreciate the dog-roses as much as she did, and the Lockhart daughters might be fast friends, if Aunt Prudence would allow it. "I am sure he would wish me to attend to our guests."

Her aunt inhaled sharply, rolling her eyes. "*My* guests— the Lockhart ladies are *my* guests, Rose. You would do well to remember your manners. Attend to your grandfather."

Disappointment sunk into Rose's stomach. Her lips parted, but she stifled the response. Arguing her case would only bring worse consequences.

Mrs. Lockhart squeezed Rose's hand. "We shall miss you very much."

Aunt Prudence stood from the sofa. "Come, she makes very little conversation. Besides, you were my friend long before my niece was ever born. Do not be so unfeeling, Rebecca."

"Forgive me, Prudence." Mrs. Lockhart released Rose's hand with marked disinclination. She gestured to her daughters. "Come, girls. Let us take a turn about the gardens with Prudence."

The four women passed by Rose, collecting their bonnets and gloves from the footmen, and left out the front door.

The empty foyer seemed to stretch on forever; isolation increased the empty space. Rose's shoulders caved forward. She did not mind visiting her grandfather. On the contrary, her readings were the highlight of her day. Rose's disappointment had far more to do with the familiar ache in the back of her throat. Mrs. Lockhart was a kind and nurturing woman, and as the closest friend of Rose's mother, Rose felt a great affection for the woman. Seeing her would have been a rare treat.

Rose swallowed, trying to dispose of her unspoken complaints. Perhaps a visit to her grandfather would be enough to lift her spirits. She climbed the grand staircase and walked down the hall of portraits to the end, where her grandfather's room lay.

Lord Josiah Grant, the Right Honorable Baron of the county, was a dutiful grandfather. At seventy-five years, Rose's grandfather was still in remarkable health, except for his eyesight. A hunting accident nineteen years prior—the very one that took Rose's father—had stolen her grandfather's sight.

With the loss of his eyesight, came the loss of freedom. Rose's grandfather had attempted, especially in her years as a child, to navigate the house on his own. He'd become quite accomplished in finding his way to the nursery, and they had spent many satisfactory days sprawled across the floor, telling stories and playing imaginary games.

Rose hesitated at the closed door. Her hand hovered over the brass handle. The last two portraits hung just feet away—those of her parents. The picture of a young woman, only seventeen at the time, never ceased to steal away Rose's breath. The woman's hair, as dark as ebony, paired exquisitely with her milky complexion and red lips.

Rose stared at the portrait with awe; her mother had been a rare beauty. It was of little wonder that her father, Augustus Grant, had fallen for her.

"Rose, is that you?" her grandfather said from the other side of the door.

She turned the knob in response. Her grandfather's impeccable hearing did not allow for much sneaking around.

"Yes, I have come for our reading." She opened the door, squinting in the darkness. "Or would you rather I come back?"

Her grandfather was as close to a father figure as she had in her life, and she adored him, but he was prone to moodiness. Rose never knew what kind of temper she might find him in.

He was strewn beneath the domed canopied bed, his back propped against two pillows. "Please, come in. I have been hoping for conversation."

The sage-colored curtains hung on both sides of the four-poster bed. Rose pulled them back, stifling a cough at the cloud of dust. "How long has it been since the maid has washed these curtains?"

Her grandfather shrugged. "Prudence thought I complained too much. She said my maid had more important rooms to attend to."

"More important rooms?" Rose clicked her tongue and moved to the window. The curtains hanging there were just as heavy material, and when they were shut, the room seemed more a dungeon than the impressive place it was made to be. She pulled them back and cracked open the window. "You are not so feeble that you must stay locked up in your bedchamber. The day is quite possibly the prettiest yet."

He laughed, the result of which sent him into a hacking cough. "You are quite right, my dear. Come, let me see you."

Rose knelt at his bedside, guiding his hands to her cheeks.

His hands brushed against her facial features, and his clouded gaze seemed to ignite. "You most likely tire of my saying so, but you have quite my son's look about you. Your nose and chin and your brows—the very same."

Rose sighed, pulling his hands to her own. "So you tell me each day."

Josiah's brows twitched. "And one day you shall see for yourself."

Since Rose's mother's passing, Aunt Prudence had ordered the removal of the entire estate's mirrors—save hers only—claiming Rose needn't become like the other silly girls of the *ton*, always doting upon their looks.

Guilt stabbed against Rose's ribs; she did so wish to see her reflection. Prudence ascribed Rose's desire to vanity, but Rose's wish had far more to do with the portraits hanging outside her grandfather's chamber. She wished to see her features as her grandfather did. Though looks had little to do with the heart, Rose often wondered if they hinted at something more. She wanted to see a piece of her mother shining back at her—and more than just her black hair.

"This day that you speak of—will it do an old man's heart some good?" her grandfather asked, pulling himself straighter against the headboard. "I hardly sense the sunlight from the darkness anymore."

Rose scowled. "What a thing to say."

He laughed. "Fetch my valet and we shall have a turn about the gardens."

Her heart swelled, and she stumbled forward to kiss his cheek. "Are you sure? It has been months since you requested such a—"

"Rose." He shook his head and pressed his fingers against her cheek. "Do not doubt the words of your elders."

She laughed, leaning against his chest. That day was decidedly the loveliest of the year—in terms of both sunlight and disposition. "Certainly. I shall call Mr. Brooks directly."

CHAPTER 2

The thundering of hooves echoed across the hillside. Wind whipped against Rose's cheeks like fiery flames, burning and brightening her fair complexion. The countryside sprawled out before her. She savored the scene, taking in each tree and patch of flowers.

Rose's mare, named Honey for the color of her coat, flew down the final slope, carrying Rose across the imaginary finish line four strides before her competitor. Rose pulled against the reins and collapsed against the horse's neck. Her heart seemed to beat out of her chest and in her ears, with each staggered breath.

She grinned, despite the stabbing pain at her side. "Well done," she said in raspy whispers, patting Honey's back. "Well done."

A young man pulled his horse to a stop beside her. His freckled face was beat red, and he swallowed before speaking. "My horse nearly tripped over that last fence. I hadn't expected you to jump."

Rose straightened in her saddle and lifted a brow at Paul.

"You thought I would follow the entire length of the fence? Have I ever been known to do such a thing?"

Her childhood friend dropped his chin to his chest and laughed. "No, but I still thought the jump rather risky. Your aunt would have never allowed me to see you again."

Silence settled between them. Aunt Prudence had already warned Rose of the risk her friendship with Paul posed to Rose's reputation.

Paul Garvey, from a neighboring cottage, had little to recommend himself—at least in the eyes of society. He was decidedly poor, with no prospects for the future, and he had not yet grown into his height nor nose. *"If only the young Mr. Garvey had looks, your association with the boy would not be so very unforgivable, but he has not a hair to recommend himself,"* Prudence had said after catching them in the gardens one morning.

"Never you mind what my aunt says. Her influence does not extend to the fields, thankfully," Rose said, lifting her eyes to meet the face of her friend. Paul was kind and good, and she considered those qualities far superior to rank or looks in matters of friendship.

He swept a hand through his disarray of curls. "No, thank goodness. I doubt she would approve of your rides, if she were to know the extent of them."

"I suppose she would disapprove of anything I choose to do." Rose clapped a hand over her mouth, and surprised laughter rolled from her lips. "I hadn't meant to say such a thing. My aunt has her good qualities."

Paul's lips twisted into a pucker, and his eyes widened. "Good qualities? Please, enlighten me, Rose. I have yet to see her say a single praise of anything—the weather, a person, a dress or reticule. The woman seems content on disparaging every possible attempt in this world."

"You are hardly around my aunt enough to know," she said, wiping at the line of perspiration near her hairline. Rose endeavored to summon a defense for her aunt, but the effort was forced and uncommonly difficult. At last, a single thought formed. "She is a most hospitable hostess."

Paul's lips trembled, and he shook with his efforts to stay his laughter. "Rose, must you speak so well about everybody all the time? I imagine the effort proves quite tiring, particularly in the case of your aunt. Why can't you say she is horrid and be done with it? Denying it, even to yourself, won't make her any better."

Her riding habit suddenly felt hot and suffocating—or perhaps it was his words. Rose blew a puff of air against her cheek, sending a stray curl from her eyes. "We shall have to agree to disagree. Now, will you tell me about your sister?"

Paul proceeded to share an account of his younger sister. Miss Lydia Garvey had been sponsored for a previous London season by a rich relative and had subsequently married a respectable gentleman from the north. Paul was eager to speak of his sister, her new home and happy situation.

Rose listened as best she could, but a nagging sensation crept into her stomach. Paul was generous in his assessment of Rose's character; she was rather tempted to speak ill of her aunt. How could she not?

After her mother's death, Aunt Prudence moved back to Grant Estate, assuming the role of mistress of the house and guardian over Rose. Since that fateful day, ten years ago, Rose's life had transformed into one of regulations and restrictions, silence and sorrow. Gone were the endless days spent in the idle play of the gardens, soft chatter at the table of Mrs. Blackburn, stories on the lap of a maternal figure, and laughter across the long dining hall.

After the ride, Rose returned Honey to her stall and hurried to the house. Time had escaped her, as it often did on her outdoor excursions, and her grandfather would be awaiting her arrival. Prudence never visited her father more than necessary, unless there was something she wished to obtain from his presence.

Rose's boots clacked against the marble entry. She handed her hat and gloves to the butler. "If my aunt should ask, I am just going up to my grandfather's room now."

Mr. Browning's eyelids twitched, and he cleared his throat, glancing toward the drawing room. "It seems you've a letter that has just arrived from Andover."

"Send it to my room. I will read the correspondence after I see to my grandfather." She spun to the staircase, lifting a foot over the first stair. She stopped when the butler cleared his throat a second time. "What is it, Mr. Browning?"

His brows drew together in a furry line. "Your aunt wishes you to read the letter now, in the drawing room."

"Oh."

Rose took a timid step toward the open room, where her aunt awaited. Dread filled her chest. Her correspondences had only recently become a matter of discussion. Another freedom had been stolen, another private affair torn to pieces—all for the sake of *propriety*.

"Rose, do come in." Aunt Prudence's voice was rigid and emotionless.

Such moments of discomfort arose often, and Rose had learned to stifle all feelings—or at least the appearance of them. She clasped her hands together and stepped into the room.

Sunlight poured into the window, illuminating the drawing room. The sofas, upholstered in a pale blue, appeared the color of the sea from the warm light; the pastels of the wall hangings seemed to take on the brilliant shades of a flower patch. The woman sitting in the corner chair sat in stark contrast to the cheeriness of the room, though her physical beauty rivaled that of any scene.

"Aunt," Rose said, curtsying.

"Your letter is on the table," Prudence said, flicking a long fingernail in the direction of the side table. "I would have read it already if not for the indecency of doing so without your presence. I pride myself on such things. Do read it aloud, child."

Rose swallowed. Was there nothing she could call her own? Her eyes fell to the signature at the bottom. "The letter is from my mother's sister, Mrs. Amelia Rolland. She writes: *Dearest Rose, I pray this letter finds you in good health. You may recall I attempted to pay a visit to you last fall, but you were gone away to Bath with your father's sister. I was saddened to have missed you and had hoped we might receive a visit from you upon your return.*"

The letter shook in her hands, and her eyes lifted to meet those of her aunt's. "My Aunt Amelia came here?"

Prudence shrugged. "I hardly thought the detail important enough to convey. I will not allow you to travel to Andover, especially to your mother's sister. She is a widow, a penniless and deprived woman. I would be shirking my duties if I were to allow you to go."

Rose's mother had not been high born; Prudence often spoke of the alliance as a disgrace, though anyone that knew Mrs. Lillian Grant had considered the baron fortunate. Rose steadied her hands at her temple. "Aunt Amelia is as deserving of my company as you and Grandfather."

"Pardon?" Prudence shifted forward in her seat. Her thin lips curled. "Deserving of your company? Do you suppose your company a reward of some sort? Far from it. Now, carry on with the letter."

Heat blistered in Rose's cheeks. She blinked furiously. Her Aunt was impossibly pernicious. Her blatant disregard for others' feelings grated against Rose like metal and rock. Rose closed her eyes, imagining the disappoint Aunt Amelia must have felt.

"The letter, child."

Nineteen was hardly a child. Rose exhaled and lifted the paper once more. *"As my oldest son, your cousin Oliver, has recently been rewarded a respectable position as head gardener for the Duke of Andover, we wish to invite you to come and stay at our cottage. In truth, we hope you will not refuse. Far too many years have passed since we have become reacquainted. Perhaps you have forgotten, but Lillian brought you to visit us on many occasions before her untimely death..."*

How could she forget? Rose had run around the countryside with her three cousins—all of which were boys—climbing trees, riding horses, even sleeping beneath the stars. Rose's mother had never seemed freer than when she was with her sister in the country. The fact that Rose had not returned to her aunt for so many years was a tragedy. Amelia used to live four hours away, but now, with Oliver's appointment, she was only a mere hour away.

"The cottage is modest, but I have a room ever at the ready. Kindly send word of your coming, day or night, and we shall be happy to receive you. Warmest regards, Your Aunt Amelia."

Rose folded the letter and pressed it to her chest. Visiting Aunt Amelia would be quite the change from Prudence's edicts. Amelia would not interfere with Rose's correspondence, restrict her from keeping friendships with the likes of Paul Garvey, nor chide her for stepping outdoors without a bonnet.

Prudence clicked her tongue. "You must write her back at once and refuse."

Rose gasped. "Grandfather would never deny me the

right." The words left her lips without a second thought. She fell back a step, shaking her head. "I only meant that I am nineteen, Aunt. I hardly need permission."

Anger flitted across Prudence's features. Her nose pinched. "You are of no age to make such decisions. Your grandfather might allow it, but he hardly cares about gossip and scandal and reputations. Such a choice would ruin your chances at a suitable match."

Matchmaking was hardly Prudence's strength. Rose had been presented with four possible suitors—all handpicked by her aunt, none of which Rose felt the slightest affections toward. Her aunt's idea of suitable seemed to include four qualities—fortune, silence, an eagerness to produce an heir, and overactive sweat glands.

Prudence lifted to a stand and shook a hand in the direction of the letter. "You will write to Amelia and refuse, or I shall write to her myself."

"No." Rose dropped her chin to her chest and sighed. "I will do so, after my reading with Grandfather."

Her aunt studied Rose for a long moment. Her lips curled into an unexpected sneer, and she placed a hand against her niece's arm. "Very well. I shall invite Mr. Higgins to call upon you tomorrow afternoon. Now, that is my idea of a match."

Rose recoiled from her aunt. Mr. Higgins was kind, but he was closer in age to her grandfather than that of a prospective husband. She could not, and would not, allow the man to entertain the idea of marriage. Some things could not be ruled, no matter how much her aunt wished it. Her heart was nonnegotiable. "Then I am free to attend your father?"

"Yes." Prudence scowled, pulling the fan from her wrist. She wafted it and wandered to the window. "I expect my father would wish to see you. He is getting rather confused in his old age, preferring the company of strange young ladies instead to that of his own daughter."

Rose turned without another word. She had far more important things to do than listen to her aunt berate her.

CHAPTER 3

$\mathcal{L}$ight blinked between the trees, casting shadows against the broken path. The edge of Grant Estate bordered along the Duke of Andover's lands, lands that were leased for agriculture purposes by tenants. The duke's properties were extensive, and the road to Andover was filled with fields and farms—all proof of the duke's fortune. But for all his property and the mere hour-proximity to her home, Rose had never met the man.

She had heard stories; her grandfather had made an off-handed remark once about Prudence's youth, alluding to her aunt's pursuit of the duke.

She reached a gap in the trees, and sunlight bore against her face. Rose closed her eyes, allowing the warmth to spread over her entire body. She pulled back her bonnet, and soft ringlets flicked across her cheek. Across the fence, somewhere past the sprawling acres and tree-lined path, Aunt Amelia lived in a cottage near the grand duke.

Rose's stomach grumbled. Her bite of toast and tea that morning was hardly enough to sustain her. She would have to turn back soon enough.

The wrath of Prudence was a certainty. Not only had Rose fled the house at first light, but she had not returned in time for Mr. Higgins's appointment. In truth, Rose contemplated returning at all. Running away from home was out of the question, but she often fantasized of doing so.

Now that her aunt Amelia lived so close, perhaps Rose might find an escape there… She sighed and shook her head. Amelia's invitation to visit was hardly a permanent offer. Further, Rose barely remembered her aunt and cousins.

Grant Estate held Rose's dearest memories, and some of the dearest people, but the shadow her aunt cast had grown darker, heavier. What once had been mere irritation and annoyance had grown into unbearable dominion.

Something had to be done…but what? Visiting her Aunt Amelia had been overruled by Prudence. Rose let out an exasperated sigh and rested against the fence. The branches overhead swayed in the wind; Rose felt much the same, swaying with her aunt's every dictate. The orders and disapproval had begun at an early age—slowly at first, but then with increasing frequency until now… Prudence claimed complete and utter control over Rose.

No mirrors, no reading by candlelight, no venturing into town without her aunt as chaperone, no participating in the musicales or public readings, no calls on other young ladies, no London season—the list was exhaustive. Worse, the reasoning behind the rules made little, if any, sense.

Yet, a cage had been built—and in part by Rose's compliance.

A lamb bleated from across the fence, and Rose held out her hand. The lamb was far from the rest of the flock. "Come little one, where is your mother? She must be worried."

Rose stepped up the bottom rung of the fence and jumped, landing squarely in a slosh of mud. Sludge reached her ankles and dirtied the hem of her pink afternoon dress.

The absurdity of the moment brought unexpected laughter. Muddied boots were the least of her concerns. Aunt Prudence posed a much more glaring problem. Something would have to be done if Rose was to ever escape her aunt's control, but for now, Rose returned her attention to the lamb. She coaxed it to the rest of the flock, patting it on the head and lifting it over divots and ledges. The duke's fields seemed remarkably untouched by time.

At last, the lamb bleated its gratitude and returned to its mother.

Rose smiled, but a pang of sadness coursed through her heart. Her mother was lost for a lifetime, but there was nothing she more desperately longed for. Longing for love was nothing new, but the dawning realization of the extent of that desire was new. She would not settle for Mr. Higgins or any other suitor her aunt threw in her direction.

Her aunt could not abide the London air, as evidenced by their short trip a few years previous. A season in London was out of the question. Rose would have to find another way to direct her efforts. Perhaps a visit to the Lockhart manor. Rebecca would be glad to have Rose, and such a visit might give Rose a chance to become better acquainted with the daughters.

"Yes, that is just the thing…" She flinched, suddenly aware she was not alone. Her attention snapped toward the movement below.

A middle-aged man stood near the quagmire at the bottom of the hill. He was watching her, a question looming in his light eyes.

She inhaled sharply. "Pardon me, sir. Your lamb was lost, and I took it upon myself to return it to the flock. Please forgive me for trespassing."

"My lamb?" He dipped his chin, and the edges of his lips

tugged. "Think nothing of it, but it is the shepherd that owes you gratitude."

"You are not...?" Her stomach twisted. The man's fashionable attire should have been enough clue; he was no shepherd. Her glance fell to his golden-stitched cuffs and the ring on his left finger. "Forgive me—"

"There is nothing to forgive. You have rescued my tenant's lamb. I daresay, this field should be leveled. The mire nearly trapped me, as evidenced by my mucked boots. I imagine animals might fall to the same fate."

Assuredness radiated from his stance and expression. Rose nearly choked on her words. "Your tenant?"

He bowed despite the ridiculousness of his situation. "The Duke of Andover, Miss—"

"Miss Rose Grant," she replied, dipping into a low curtsy. "Your Grace."

"Please, do stand. Our meeting has done away with formality, and you have rescued my tenant's lamb."

She straightened. Of all times to meet the grand duke. Her cheeks burned in embarrassment. She knew not where to look —and her hands? She placed them at her side, then clasped them together in an awkward attempt to appear at ease.

He tapped a gloved finger against his chin. "Grant...a relative of the Honorable Josiah Grant?"

Rose nodded tentatively. "Josiah is my grandfather, Your Grace."

"Is he?" A smiled brightened the duke's features. "I do believe I have met your parents, Augustus Grant and Lillian Parson. I am ashamed I did not recognize your looks sooner —your likeness is remarkable."

Rose's eyes widened. "You knew them?"

He removed his hat, revealing a large mop of graying hair. "Yes, particularly well. In those days, I attended some of the

same parties as your father, danced with the same partners...
vied for one particular woman's attention."

Rose's grandfather had never mentioned as much. A
blush overtook her entire face. What was there to say in such
a situation? Polite responses played across her mind, but a
familiar nagging pulled at her. "I find it strange to meet those
of my parents' former acquaintance."

"Oh?" he asked, stepping even closer. "And why is that?"

She shook her head, inwardly chiding herself for
speaking so freely. "The same blood that flowed through my
father and mother flows through me, Your Grace, but I know
nothing of my father—not by experience anyway, and my
mother died when I was a child. But you...I suspect from
your smile that you know a great deal about them both."

"Your suspicions are correct. I did know them both well,
Miss Grant, and I am sorry for your loss."

She dropped her gaze. The field was a mixture of grasses and
flowers, rocks and ridges, shrubbery and sloshes of mud. In
nature, variance was to be admired. But in life? Rose had often
wished for the life of those around her—life with parents, a
sister or brother, even a house pet. Dwelling on such details
never ended with anything other than heartache, and so Rose
pushed away the thoughts—as she always did when they came—
and returned her attention to the duke. "Thank you, Your Grace.
What brings you to our village this morning? I have never
chanced upon you in this field before, and I take this walk often."

A smile stole across his cheeks, and wrinkles appeared at
the corners of his eyes. Rose imagined her father would have
been close to the duke's age. "I seemed to have lost my way,
Miss Grant. I am ashamed to admit it, but my horse threw
me, and I have been wandering the countryside for hours."

"You are lost?" Rose gasped. "Please, allow me to assist
you. Where are you expected?"

The duke's laughter rolled across the space between them. "The situation is undeniably amusing, though I beg you would not utter a word of this meeting to a soul." He leaned against a nearby boulder to catch his breath. "I am past expected at the home of a Mr. Bagshaw."

Mr. Matthew Bagshaw, a respected farmer, lived nearly ten miles from where they stood. "And you are without your horse? That is—you have lost him entirely?"

"Yes, unfortunately." He folded his arms across his chest.

"Would you be opposed if I offered to help, Your Grace? My home is only two miles away, and you could have your pick of horses to borrow. My grandfather would be honored to be of service." Rose held in a breath. She did not know what was worse—offering assistance to the duke or leaving him to his own resources. Her hands grew cold and clammy, and she tore them apart and wiped them against the front of her dress.

He surveyed her silently. There was caution in his gaze, and something else, though Rose could not decipher it. "Does your aunt reside on the property?"

Understanding flickered to her eyes. If the stories Rose's grandfather told were correct, the situation would be unbearably uncomfortable for both the duke and Prudence. No wonder Rose had not met him prior. "Yes, my aunt is at home, though I should think she would also be happy to assist you."

His eyes darted around the ground as if he were searching for something. He pressed a palm to his waistcoat, fluttering his fingers about until they landed on his handkerchief. He pressed the fabric to his brow. "Quite right, Miss Grant. I regret to trespass upon your hospitality, but I do not see another way out of my predicament."

Rose offered a timid smile. She understood the man's

anxiety all too well; her aunt had a knack for bringing about such worry.

He extended his arm and sighed. "Then will you walk with me?"

She took his arm and led him across the pasture. She blushed when she climbed the fence, acutely aware of how improper the movement was in such a dress.

The duke only smiled, and his eyes seemed to brighten. "I shall not tell a soul, Miss Grant. It seems you and I both have secrets to bury."

Rose laughed in response.

The path followed the property lines for some time, and the odd pair fell into easy conversation. At first, they discussed the spring blossoms on the neighboring hill and the impressive size of the trees lining the fence, but as time wore on, the duke began to speak of his son Colin and ask after Rose's childhood, her grandfather, and the prospects for her future.

The words caught in her throat at first. Rose had struggled to explain away so much of her past. Speaking to anyone about such topics would have been difficult—but the duke? However, once loosed, her tongue spun off memories and stories as quickly as their feet carried them across the distances. With each recollection, a weight lifted, and Rose felt surprisingly free in the man's presence.

Kindness shone from his expression. "I remember my first meeting with your mother."

She stopped, staring up at his face. The portrait hanging in the hall haunted her thoughts. Rose's mother was strikingly beautiful, the memories of her even sweeter. Yet, Rose questioned whether time and longing had more to do with the recollections. "Truly? Will you tell me? I have only a handful of memories, and I worry I am painting an entirely abstract portrait of her."

The duke's brows crinkled, and his lips parted. "I doubt so. Your mother was unforgettable." He paused to smile. "I met her in Andover. I rarely was permitted to traipse around town unattended, but I had escaped that day—much to the chagrin of my mother. I took to the small shops and fancied I was indistinguishable among the other customers."

The image of him as a young man, pretending to be anything other than a duke was undeniably comical. Rose's lips tugged. "Then you were not always so composed and grand?"

Laughter split his lips apart. "I do believe you are teasing, Miss Grant, but I will not be derailed. Your mother was standing just outside the dress shop. I remember well her beauty. I determined I would introduce myself to her chaperone, but nerves overcame me. Later, perhaps months, I met her again at a ball. This time, I had deduced her identity and knew she was but the daughter of a dressmaker. Yet, I begged three dances of her that night."

Rose's mouth gaped open. "You did not!"

"I did." He winked. "Though, my efforts were too little and too late. Another man, the son of the Honorable Josiah Grant, had already stolen her affection. I was left to mourn my own idiocy."

"You are kind to tell me the story," Rose said, smiling up at him. "I believe you are right. My father stole her affection quite quickly, from their first encounter I am told. Her beauty and character must have been impressive. To garner so much attention..."

The duke exhaled. "She was, and she did."

"Thank you." Rose released his arm.

He cleared his throat. "I do believe things worked out just as they were meant to be. Your mother may have slipped away from me, but then—I never would have met my duchess. Mary has been the ideal wife, and we share three children."

They stopped below the front steps of the estate. Rose could not recall a more enjoyable stroll. She climbed the steps. "I imagine you are happy then, Your Grace."

"I am." He dipped his chin. "And for that I am thankful."

At their arrival, the footman opened the large mahogany door.

Rose led the duke inside and gestured to the drawing room. "If you will, Your Grace. I will bring you paper and ink so that you might write—"

"Rose Margaret Grant, I simply cannot forgive you," Aunt Prudence's ear-piercing voice echoed from above. She stood at the top of the staircase, hands against her hips. Her lips nearly disappeared in her tight expression. "Mr. Higgins waited for you for nearly an hour. To think I raised you better than that!"

Rose nearly stumbled. Tension coiled inside her stomach. Prudence's berating was expected, but the presence of the duke only heightened Rose's humiliation. "I am sorry for my absence, but I—"

"But nothing. You will stay to your room and go without supper." Her aunt lifted her chin. "Perhaps then you will understand the difficult position you placed me in. Mr. Higgins will not want anything to do with you now, and he was quite the catch."

Rose's stomach complained already, and she longed for a slice of Mrs. Blackburn's cake. "As you wish, but I must attend to our guest, Aunt."

"Our guest?" Prudence descended a few steps, and her face flooded with color as she caught a glimpse of the duke.

"Good day, Mrs. Grant. I fear it has been years since we last met." The duke's eyes narrowed. "I do ask you not punish your niece so severely. She has come to my aid, and I owe her my deepest gratitude."

Prudence's eyes widened, and panic etched into her trembling limbs. She nearly slid down the steps, falling into a deep curtsy at the bottom stair. "Your Grace. Pardon my temper. It was concern that caused the scolding."

He smirked. "If you claim so. Now, Miss Grant," he said. His eyes softened in an instant, and he stepped toward the drawing room. "A paper and ink would do splendidly. My son will be worried."

Rose nodded. "Yes, Your Grace." She moved past her aunt, who was still bent at the bottom of the stairs. "Shall I also ask about a horse?"

His gaze snapped back to Prudence's crimson face. "I think not. On second thought, I shall send for my carriage to collect me. It seems your aunt and I have much to discuss."

Rose's heart beat in an irregular fashion, pounding then slowing to an indeterminable speed. The duke remained in the drawing room with Aunt Prudence, discussing something rather serious by the sounds of it. Every so often, Rose heard the low rumble of the duke's voice and her aunt's particularly high-pitched and nasally responses. *"You are not her guardian." "I have only her best interest at heart." "You cannot understand the difficulties such a child poses."*

Rose winced. The duke seemed to have taken it upon himself to act as her protector. Unbeknownst to him, his efforts would only hurt Rose further. Aunt Prudence's anger was not to be trifled with. Yet, her heart softened. The duke was too kind, especially considering their unusual and recent meeting.

The latch of the drawing room sounded, and the door

swung open. The duke stood in the entrance. He smiled when he met Rose's bowed head. "Miss Grant, your aunt and I were just discussing how you must take a season in London."

"A season?" Rose's eyes widened. "But my aunt cannot abide the air, Your Grace. She has forbidden it."

He nodded. "So she explained, though I insisted. Miss Grant, you cannot stay locked up in this home—however beautiful it is. Your chances of a suitable match are nonexistent here. No Mr. Higgins or Mr. Flock will do. You are young, and I have informed your aunt of my cousin, Mrs. Bridges. She would be more than willing to sponsor you. She has never had a daughter, you see."

The next season was nearly five months away, but possibilities danced across Rose's mind with increasing speed. Her mouth parted into a smile. Emotion threatened. She could not remember the last time someone had been so considerate. "Your Grace," she said, her voice shaking, "Thank you."

He took her hand. "A pleasure, I assure you, Miss Grant. Now—"

A rap against the door sounded, and the footman opened it.

"Pardon, I have come to collect my father, the Duke of Andover," came a deep voice.

"Colin, you are right on time," the duke said in response. He chuckled. "But first you must meet the charming Miss Rose Grant. She saved me from an aimless wander."

The duke's son, the Marquess of Stratfordshire, took a step into the foyer, and Rose's heart stopped altogether. He dipped his chin in greeting. "An introduction would be marvelous, Father. I have spent the better half of the morning searching for you."

Rose was unprepared for such a sight. His chiseled jaw and large smile were only upstaged by his eyes. They were

28

the color of a tempest-torn sea, with splashes of blue and green swirled into an intoxicating blend. Words escaped her, and she managed a wobbly curtsy. "My Lord."

The duke studied her expression, and a soft smile sprawled across it. "My son, Miss Grant—Lord Stratford-shire. He has the good fortune of taking after his mother in looks, though I claim a small victory in owning his stature."

Rose lifted her gaze to Colin once more.

His widened gaze rested upon her with seemingly surprised admiration. He bowed. "Miss Grant, please allow me to thank you."

"My niece only did what was expected, My Lord." Aunt Prudence had risen from the sofa and come to the foyer. Her cheeks were pink and her eyes puffy. No doubt, she had been crying from her discussion with the duke, but her expression had turned cold and rigid once more. She clicked her tongue. "But we are honored with your presence."

"Are you?" the duke asked, lips trembling.

Curiosity piqued. Whatever had passed between them in their youth had soured over time. The duke hardly attempted at civility, though his attentions to Rose were unfalteringly warm.

Rose turned to Colin. "Have you found the horse, Lord Stratfordshire?"

Colin shook his head slightly, and his dark waves shifted. "Not yet, but my servants are endeavoring to do so as we speak."

Concern knit in Rose's brows. The poor animal was undoubtedly frightened. "I take walks daily. If perchance—"

"I shall inform you at once if we are to see the creature," Prudence said, stepping between Rose and Colin. Her voice grew flat and unmistakably dry. "If you should need anything else, I am happy to comply. It is not every day we are honored with the presence of a duke and marquess."

The duke stole Rose's hand once more, bowing over it. "Miss Grant."

She curtsied in response. "Your Grace."

Colin followed suit, and when Rose met his glance, she was once more taken aback by the magnificence of his stare. His eyes were like nothing she had seen before. She was ashamed to admit the emotions pulsing through her. Perhaps Prudence was right in removing the mirrors from the house. If the duke's son could cause such affectation by a mere glance, Rose had fallen prey to vainness and the shallowest of effects.

* * *

THE DUKE, seated in the carriage across from his son, waited for a few moments to speak. "A diverting day to be sure."

Colin shook his head. From his father's slight smile and beaming gaze, Colin suspected the duke was up to his usual mischief. The fact that the duke had not sustained injuries from falling from his horse was a miracle. Colin would have been devastated if tragedy had befallen his father; he needed him. "I told you to take someone with you, but you insisted on riding the lands alone. Why?"

"For the same reason you refuse to take someone along on your rides. I enjoy solitude—and none so much as when I am on the back of a horse. Besides, have you ever met a more charming young woman?"

Colin smiled in disbelief. "You mean the younger Miss Grant?"

Rose's beauty was impossible to miss. Dark hair, paired with light skin and hazel eyes, was rare indeed. At first glance, she was breathtakingly handsome. Yet, beauty in and of itself was common enough. Colin had seen more than his fair share of pretty women, and each one seemed interested in only two things—title and fortune.

"Tell me, Father, what makes Miss Grant different than the rest of the ladies we entertain?" Colin asked, stroking his chin.

The duke chuckled. He leaned back against the carriage cushion and sighed. "When you get to be my age, son, you learn to notice the subtle. Rose is much like her mother—uncommonly kind and unaware of her own loveliness. Prudence has been hiding her away. I am sure of it."

The muscles along Colin's jaw tightened. He well remembered the stories of Miss Prudence Grant. She had vied for his father's affection as a young debutante. She had attempted to ensnare the duke on multiple occasions, and she exhibited every jealous inclination known to the *ton*. His father often spoke of her when warning Colin.

"You have the tendency of putting too much faith in first impressions, Father. Miss Grant may well be as conniving and sinister as her aunt." But even as he spoke the words, Colin did not believe them. Instinct favored Rose more than he wished to admit. There was something genuine about her gaze and expressions.

"No." The duke shook his head vehemently. His lips fell to a frown. "When I came upon Miss Grant, she did not know my identity. She quite ridiculously mistook me for a shepherd and apologized for trespassing—though she had only done so to save a poor bleating lamb."

The carriage swayed, and the sound of wheels against gravel filled the sudden silence.

Colin was to marry; his father thought it time. At five and twenty, Colin even wished to find a suitable lady. Yet, finding a worthy woman proved difficult. He did not naively expect a love match; enduring friendship was the most Colin hoped for, considering his wealth and titles.

The duke believed it his duty to assist Colin in the search for a proper wife, but so far, Colin had not felt the least inclination in his father's suggestions. Rose, however, had sparked interest in their brief meeting.

"Colin…" His father leaned forward in his seat, setting his hands against his knees. "I understand your hesitancy. I have been there. I do think you would get on with Miss Grant rather nicely. Do me the honor of calling upon her tomorrow. You may even use the horse as an excuse. Will you consider that much?"

"If that is your wish, Father."

The duke chuckled once more. His shoulders shook with the effort. "I see you are quick to appease me on this matter."

Colin's lips tugged. He hardly needed to encourage his father's teasing, but Colin could not resist adding, "Ever the dutiful son."

"Quite. Now, there is a lovely patch of gardens on the estate. Perhaps you will ask her for a ride—or a walk, if you are so inclined?"

Goodness. His father was likely to plan the entire wedding if Colin did not say something. He cleared his throat and repressed a smile. "And what of discussion? Have you considered everything I should ask and say?"

The duke's eyes lit with amusement. "I see what you are getting at. I will refrain from directing your efforts further, so long as you do call on Miss Grant…?"

Colin turned to look out the window. "Have I ever acted against your edicts?"

"Not ever," his father said in a serious tone. "Not ever, Colin."

CHAPTER 4

*T*he pail dropped into the well, splashing when it reached the bottom. Rose leaned over the ledge, staring into the hole. The sun bore down, and a glimmer of a reflection shone back at her.

Aunt Prudence had gone to drastic measures to keep Rose from seeing her reflection, all under the guise of modesty. Rose hadn't questioned the method, until the last two years. She had caught glimpses of herself in the reflection of silver pitchers, marbled glass, the pond beyond the flower garden, and the shadowed outline of her profile in the sunlight. But every attempt resulted in distorted images, each stretching and pulling her features into a picture that only a child might sketch.

She ran her fingers across her cheeks and brows, endeavoring to see like her grandfather—with touch—but nothing satisfying resulted from the effort. She sighed, pulling back the bucket of water. She spun her fingers in the liquid, humming softly.

Boots against the gravel caught her ears, and she straightened in an instant.

"Miss Grant?"

She peered around the kitchen garden archway and saw the outline of the Marquess of Stratfordshire. Her mouth went dry. She had not expected to see him again, at least not until her season next fall. Their meeting yesterday had left her with a restless sleep.

Nervousness spun her mind, and her hands trembled. "Lord Stratfordshire," she managed, stepping forward to meet him.

Colin's expression held a question. "My father sent me to inquire after his horse. I asked after you, but your aunt insisted you were not at home. I see she was misinformed…"

"Yes, misinformed." Rose smiled and curtsied.

"My father also told me about the charming gardens on your estate and suggested I ask you for a ride. I am currently directing some improvements in our gardens in Andover, and my father seems to think your land worthy inspiration." His cheeks held the slightest blush, and his posture faltered. "But I would not wish to impose upon your solitude."

She shook her head, and she swallowed. Their meeting the previous day, though brief, had summoned new sensations—ones Rose had not known existed. She felt entirely ridiculous for her attraction to Colin. He was a marquess, set to inherit a dukedom.

"Shall I return another day then?" he asked, looking past her into the kitchen garden.

Her senses returned, and she shook her head once more. "A walk would be most enjoyable this time of day, My Lord. Shall I fetch my groom and a pair of horses?"

His cheeks darkened another shade. "I must admit I have already taken upon myself the liberty of doing so. When I was about to depart, I saw you sitting through the archway."

Unexpected delight caught her breath. Rose took fifteen minutes to change into her riding habits and boots. She returned and took Colin down the same path she had taken with the duke, stopping every so often to point out an arrangement of plants.

When they reached the pond, they dismounted, and Rose stopped to pick a few flowers.

Colin took a few rocks from the ground, skipping them across the water with unanticipated adeptness.

She tucked the stems of her recently picked flowers into her pocket and allowed herself to study the man beside her. The marquess was more than handsome; he was captivating. His manners were polished beyond measure. Even his posture commanded attention. Colin seemed like a portrait hanging in a hall—splendid and regal, attractive, and the very definition of an upstanding gentleman. But his eyes—she dared to glance at them once more. His eyes hinted at something more, something buried deep beneath the manners and expectations.

"Do you enjoy riding for sport, My Lord?" she asked. The desire to see the truth behind the man at her side struck her with startling force.

"Yes, more than anything." He faced her, and the effect sent a wave of warmth to her chest.

She flicked her chin toward the field opposite the pond. "There is a particularly pleasant piece of land just past the trees. You must ride the path on your next trip to your tenant lands."

The marquess's lips parted in seeming surprise. A fire ignited between the green and blue of his eyes. "I would be glad to *today*, if you are willing."

Rose blushed. She had not intended the idea as an invitation. Rather, she had asked about riding in an attempt at understanding his character. "If that would please you."

They took to the beaten-down path, and Rose led him through the canopy of trees until they reached the clearing.

Sunlight illuminated the scene of wildflowers, broken up only by a few trees and the occasional rocks. The path, from years of use by Rose and Paul, had turned to dirt.

Rose pulled back her reins and turned to Colin. "If you are up for sport—"

"Far more than I appear," he said, interrupting. He grinned for the first time that day, and a charming line near the left edge of his lips deepened, revealing a complimenting dimple. The effect was an entirely unfair advantage. "Please, lead the way, Miss Grant."

Something told her Colin was a more formidable opponent than Paul Garvey. She took in a slow breath, fixating on the marquess's dimple. "Very well."

Rose kicked her horse to an impressive sprint. The warm air beat against her, tugging loose her chignon.

Colin kept his stallion even with Rose's horse.

Rose pushed Honey harder. She stifled her laughter. Racing the duke's son was perhaps the most absurd thing she had ever done. Her entire upbringing told her to allow Colin to win. Injuring his pride would not serve either of them. Yet, Rose's hands tightened on the reins, and she crouched forward, flying across the path at top speed.

A smile crept over her lips when she spied the fallen logs ahead. She jumped with precision, landing briefly before jumping another set of obstacles.

When they finally stopped for breath, they joined together in laughter.

"My father told me you were a unique lady, Miss Grant, but I am ashamed I did not understand his meaning. I think I have repented on that account," Colin said, stroking his stallion's back. "I have hardly met your equal in the saddle."

Rose dismounted, leading her horse back the way they had come. She sent a mock-warning glance at the marquess. "I will forgive you, Lord Stratfordshire, if you will not breathe a word of this to anyone. My aunt detests when I ride so wildly."

"My father warned me you were a woman of secrets."

Rose's jaw dropped. "Your father—he promised not to speak of my climbing that fence."

Colin bit his bottom lip, and his dimple manifested itself once more. "Yes, so he said, but then again—you cannot fault him. I was already privy to his being thrown from the horse and his embarrassing plight of enlisting a young woman for directions. Besides, I believe I have seen much more incriminating evidence of your shocking behavior."

Her cheeks ached from smiling. "Shocking? I doubt anything is as shocking as seeing the Marquess of Stratfordshire racing an innocent young lady."

Colin's deep laughter returned. "I suppose that was rather bad form, wasn't it? My father assures me you are rather good at keeping secrets though."

Rose nodded. "I imagine we are both bound to secrecy. The poor groom was left, quite abruptly. Benson must be shaking his head as we speak, berating our behavior."

"Then Benson is like my nurse. She was always scolding me for childish fancies—climbing trees, running, riding the most spirited horses."

"You mean she disliked you to act as a child?" Rose asked, remembering her own childhood adventures. Rose would have lived outdoors had it been acceptable.

Colin's expression flattened. "I suppose childhood is not reserved for those of nobility. A future duke is not allowed to indulge such whims."

Rose halted. "I think our lives a foil, Lord Stratfordshire. My childhood was the only freedom I have known, while your freedom seems to have only recently arrived."

"You think I am free now?" Colin shook his head, and his

dark brows drew down. "Hardly. My duties dictate so much of my life—"

"But you are happy, and that is more freedom than most. Your father admires you, or so it seemed from our discussion yesterday. That must bring internal freedom of sorts. I cannot imagine not competing for my aunt's approval. The effort is futile, and I do not understand why I continue to labor for it."

Colin chewed on the inside of his cheek, seeming to contemplate for a long moment. "My father is under the impression that your aunt is punishing you for things out of your control."

Rose closed her eyes. Prudence had grievance enough with Rose, not to mention jealousies concerning the baron's affections, but what had the duke told Colin? Rose tugged on a loose curl. "I cannot believe my aunt would be so cruel."

"Forgive me. My father warned me that you were uncommonly charming, and that familiarity would come as a result of your very presence. I should not speak of such things."

Rose released a slow breath. She could not fault Colin. He seemed much like his father, willing to come to her defense after momentary acquaintance. "Your father has shown me greater kindness than most. He seems to have exaggerated my good character."

Colin's lip twitched. "He admired your mother very much, and he claims you are much like her."

Emotion jolted her. "He said that?"

"Yes."

Rose's breath turned shallow. She had longed to hear that, to feel as if a piece of her mother remained in her character, in her words and laughter. "I believe the horses are sufficiently rested, Lord Stratfordshire. Shall we ride again?"

He mounted without another word, and the pair of them rode in relative silence. But conversation, once they reached the stables and walked to the front of the house, quickly found its way between them once more.

Rose curtsied, offering a smile. "I hope you are not too worn-out for your return ride."

A flicker of sunlight lit his eyes. Since their return to the groom, the marquess had resumed his mannered and guarded expressions. Even his posture had turned practiced, but Rose was happy to see his gaze still held a semblance of unrestraint. "If anything, my time on your land was invigorating. Thank you for the tour, Miss Grant. I am attending a musicale at the Ainsworth's estate in two days, just north of here. I shall write to them and request your presence, if you would be so inclined?"

Her voice grew airy. "I will try, My Lord."

"Until then." He bowed and took to his horse.

Rose watched him ride into the distance, until his figure was nothing more than a speck along the distant hills. Colin had awoken something within her. She felt more alive in his presence, and conversation came much like it did with the duke—easily and comfortably. Only, Rose was certain she felt something quite different for the marquess than that of the duke. The duke evoked endearment, while Colin brought about something deeper—and slightly more alarming; Rose had never felt anything more than platonic kindness toward those in her circle.

Lord Stratfordshire inspired admiration.

"Getting on with the marquess, I see."

Rose whipped around.

Aunt Prudence stood on the steps, tapping her fan against a hand. "That will never do, Rose. You have nothing to offer a man of his station. Take it from me; dukes want nothing to do with Grant women. Now, wash up before dinner and change from that abominable habit."

Rose's shoulders caved forward. Her aunt was spiteful;

yet, her words cut through Rose's euphoria, slicing deeper into her insecurities. Did Rose have anything to offer a man of rank—or any man at all? Besides horse rides and walks around the garden, Rose imagined her company dull and insufficient; at least it had proven so to her aunt.

Rose took the steps, two at a time, and passed by her aunt. She refused to meet Prudence's eyes. Why could Rose never seem to do anything right? Sadness sunk into Rose's throat, rising to her downturned lips and suddenly glistening eyes. She could not decide which was worse, Prudence's perpetual disappointment in Rose or her aunt's cruelty.

"Do not be late for dinner, child," Aunt Prudence mumbled. "I suspect we shall need to discuss the musicale."

"The—" Rose halted at the house threshold. Emotion crept into her voice, and she grasped the side of the open door for support. "You have never allowed me to attend mus—"

"We shall discuss it. I do not think it wise to reject the invitation of the marquess, no matter my opinion on the spectacles. I suggest you change and hurry. Dinner will begin as usual."

Guilt knocked against Rose's chest. She reeled backward, and the shame of her momentary judgement sent tears down her cheeks. How could she have been so quick to assign Prudence malicious intent? "Oh, Aunt. Thank you."

Prudence cleared her throat. "Dinner."

Rose nodded and hurried to her bedchamber.

* * *

COLIN'S HORSE sped across the fields to Andover. Trees blended together in passing; rocks and ridges rose and fell at a surprising rate, but he doubted there was a more attractive stretch of land in all of Hampshire.

Thank goodness for that ground below; it was quite possibly the only thing keeping him anchored to the present. The duke had been conservative in his assessment of Rose's character; she far surpassed Colin's idea of pleasant company. Their conversation, slow at first, had increased considerably after the ride.

That ride.

A grin stretched across his cheeks. Colin was delighted to find a kinship with Rose; her practiced smiles and conversation carried secrets as well, not the least of which included an adventurous spirit.

Rose was more than courageous; she allowed herself to become one with the horse, an act that required confidence and trust. Her laughter still rang in his ears, and Colin hoped to keep hold of the sound until their next meeting. One pleasant afternoon did not guarantee compatibility, but the meeting was a promising start.

The late afternoon sun lit the estate in the distance. Colin exhaled and admired the shape of the rooflines, the trees along the drive, the ever-comforting smell of lilacs, and the chirping of birds. He could never tire of such sights, sounds, and smells, for they ran through his memories like a well-worn book—continuously comforting, infinitely satisfying, and heartwarmingly familiar.

For nearly four generations, the Dukes of Andover had resided at Stratfordshire. Colin stood to inherit the title and the lands after his father passed on. But no matter how he endeavored to prepare himself for such a charge, the idea left a hole in his chest. Duty or not—Colin did not wish to consider his future without his father at his side.

Colin slowed his stallion, steadying his breath. A figure came in to view, and as Colin approached, the figure of the duchess took shape.

"Mother," he said, tipping his hat.

She carried a basket in her arms, most likely from some charitable errand. Her gaze brightened at the sight of her son, and she smiled. "Colin, you've come back. Your father said you meant to call upon some acquaintances."

"And you? Have you gone to the Smith family again?" Colin asked.

She tucked a strand of silver-blonde hair into her bonnet. Such serviceable outings were hardly expected of a duchess. From the gossip that reached Colin, some even believed the duchess improper in taking up such menial tasks. "Yes. I believe their little boy is improving, but I cannot be sure. I will send Doctor Clark to the house later."

He dipped his chin. His mother was thoughtful, almost to a fault. Colin could not recall the last time she had taken care of her own nerves or health. The duchess's constant cough worried Colin. Doctor Clark seemed incapable of providing a cure; though to be fair, Colin blamed fate more than the physician.

Colin dismounted, walking beside his mother. He towered over her petite frame. "And your walk? Did you take care?"

Upon closer inspection, her cheeks held the slightest pink. She brushed a hand against his arm. "I am well enough, son. Now, tell me about your outing. Did you see anyone I might know?"

"No, I am afraid I did not visit anyone that you know"—Colin took a breath to add emphasis—"yet."

The duchess's brow lifted. "Oh?"

He grasped her hand, wrapping it around his arm. "Miss Rose Grant, Lord Josiah Grant's granddaughter. They live only—"

"I know of Josiah."

Colin shuffled against the gravel. As a rule, his mother did not interrupt. Frankly, the duchess did not do anything that was deemed unmannerly or unkind. He swallowed. "And... I assume by your clipped tone—you do not approve of the man."

She sighed, waiting for a minute to speak. "It is not that I dislike Lord Grant. He was always kind enough, and I feel the utmost compassion for his accident those years ago. It is only..."

"Yes?" Collin stopped, stepping in front of her. He took her hands in his. "What is it, Mother?"

"His son married a Miss Lillian... Parson, I believe. I understand many men were quite taken with her. Is the daughter, Miss Grant, similar?" Her lips fell to a frown.

Colin shrugged. "I never met the lady in question, but Father says as much." He bit down on his bottom lip, realizing his mistake. For all the duke's mention of Rose's mother throughout the years, Colin doubted his mother had not recognized the admiration in his voice. "At least he suspects. He does not know Miss Grant well. They only met yesterday after he was thrown from his horse."

Any trace of sadness seemed to vanish from her expression, and she nodded. "Then you must tell me; what is Miss Grant like?"

"She is a quiet girl, at least at first. She seems to be genuinely good natured, despite her aunt's ridiculous demands." Colin lifted a finger to silence his mother's questions. The subject of Prudence would have to wait. "But, after a short moment, I found her conversation quite pleasant. She seems to enjoy riding and touring gardens almost as much as I do. Her eyes—I would be hard-pressed to name a lady with finer ones, and her laugh..."

A blush crept over him, and Colin snickered. He sounded just as jumbled and confused as he felt. Nothing made sense about his feelings, not yet at least. Miss Grant's acquaintance was new. "Forgive me. I am far too excited from my ride."

The duchess's eyes widened. "Smitten already, Colin? Do take care, son."

"You are right, of course, Mother." Colin dropped his chin to his chest. "But in any case, I hope you will not mind if I invite Miss Grant and her aunt to the musicale at the Ainsworth's estate?"

She shook her head, coughing into her hand. "I would be happy to meet her, especially if she is as enchanting as you describe. I have often wondered what type of woman is capable of catching your eye."

He winced.

"It is only that, in the past years, you seemed immune to the charms of every girl who batted her eyes at you, only to be smitten in an instant with Miss Grant. I am curious, and, as always, hopeful for your happiness."

There was no denying the worry lacing his mother's words. Fortune and status hunters were common enough, and pretty girls without a thought of their own were an even sadder fate. But more alarming, was the possibility of heart-break. For with the surge of eagerness and curiosity, came a startling reality; Rose had the power to crush Colin's pride—if not his growing affection.

He took a steady step, calling to mind every lesson on composure he had received. He would follow his mother's advice; he would take care. And yet, Colin could not suppress a smile. He needed to write to Mr. Ainsworth straight away to request an invitation for Miss Grant and her aunt. He needed to see Rose again.

CHAPTER 5

The anticipation of seeing the marquess again only increased in the two days that followed. Rose found herself, admittedly more often than not, contemplating their ride and conversation. A smile rose to her cheeks each time she thought of his sea-colored eyes or the way a smile transformed Colin into an entirely different person.

She stared at the blank wall, while her maid worked on the task at hand—managing Rose's tangle of dark waves. From the exasperated sounds behind her, Rose gathered the chore was not going as planned. She tapped her fingers on the dressing table and looked at the bouquet of flowers.

She adored flowers. Her mother had often gone by the nickname 'Lilly'. So when Rose, at only four years old, realized her good fortune of also taking the name of a flower, she had been eager to tell her mother. *You and I are a pair of flowers, Mama,* she had said. Rose's mother had giggled in response, *"Yes, but the loveliest addition to that of any bouquet is that of a rose, my dear."*

Rose cleared her throat. "Would you be so kind as to put a few flowers in my hair, Kate?"

The maid's fingers fell to Rose's shoulders. "A lovely choice, Miss Grant. Shall I place a few of the white ones, or would you prefer the purple?"

Rose fumbled through the arrangement, plucking out an assortment. "Here, take what you consider best."

Kate worked a few of the flowers into Rose's hair, pinning and prodding, in utter silence.

Aunt Prudence had been clear of how the staff were to be handled; they were not to be treated with the familiarity that many masters mistakenly offered. Compliance proved a struggle. Rose wished to ask Kate, and the other servants, questions; she longed for a confidante and friend.

However, Rose reluctantly obeyed her aunt, clamping her mouth shut with every impulsive wish.

Laura, another servant, stood at the doorway, carrying the newly pressed evening gown. The pale green and silk sleeves glistened under the lantern light, and the delicate sheer fabric overlay of the skirt swished from the movement. "Your dress, Miss Grant."

Rose smiled. Her grandfather had gifted her the dress—left to the dressmaker's artistry—for her most recent birthday. The garment had hung in her armoire for nearly five months untouched; she had not had occasion to wear it. "You may set it on the bed. Thank you, Laura."

Aunt Prudence appeared in the doorway, watching as Laura set down the gown. Her lips twitched. "Your grandfather will be pleased to know you are wearing the new dress. I also wish to bestow a gift."

Rose's head shot up. Her aunt had never given anything other than a scolding. "For me?"

Prudence nodded. She pulled out something from behind her back. The undergarment was far longer than the normal

46

stay, with more intricate lacing and ribbing. "To keep you in perfect form and posture, my dear."

Dread stabbed at Rose's stomach. She had seen such contraptions, though few women still suffered such torture. The current fashion of dresses, with empire waists, hardly called for such measures. And to think of singing in such an uncomfortable state. "But I am to perform at the musicale."

"And you shall." Prudence's gaze narrowed. She flicked her head at Kate. "I think Miss Grant's hair is more than ready. You may return to your room. I will assist her in dressing." She directed Rose to stand and wrapped the corset around her middle. "Your first musicale—and in the presence of the duke and duchess! You must feel very honored, as I do to be accompanying you this evening. Now, do not utter a word unless spoken to."

Rose gasped just as Prudence pulled the strings. With her aunt's force, Rose's ribs were liable to crack. She winced in pain. "Please, I can scarcely breathe."

"Just so. It is much better to be seen than to breathe."

To Rose's dismay, the strings were pulled again and again, until her waist had decreased to the size of a child's. Rose shoulders drew backward. Settling her shallow breaths took all her concentration. She needed no advice on speaking; Rose could scarcely utter a word under such confines. Singing would be near impossible.

Prudence whipped the laces back and forth, tying them with surprising enthusiasm. "There, now you are fit to be seen. Now, for the dress—"

Rose lifted her arms, allowing Prudence to put on the dress.

"Why so pale, child?"

Rose shook her head and attempted at a smile. Attending a musicale, even in uncomfortable attire, was infinitely preferable to the isolation of her home. Seeing Colin again was worth enduring any discomfort. "I am well. Thank you."

Prudence's left brow lifted slightly. "Well then, let us go down to the carriage."

The ride took over an hour, and Rose felt every excruciating bump along the road. The ribbing of the corset jabbed into her sides and hips, and with each bounce of the carriage, Rose was sent one way or another, unable to control her center of balance.

If not for the view out the window, the journey would have been insufferable. As they approached the Ainsworth residence, Milton Manor, the golden sun of evening illuminated each flower and stray blade of glass along the drive. Rose stifled a smile; her aunt detested excited displays. Yet, with each stride of the horses, the restraint of the corset lessened. Her breathing steadied. She would see the marquess again, and something about that fact brought immense joy— as if the golden sun shone straight through the carriage and into her heart.

The driver slowed the horses, and the wheels creaked to a stop in front of the stone estate.

Rose gasped. The house, built two centuries ago in the Tudor style, stretched at least four stories high. Layers of gray stone, each meticulously carved and cut into place by craftsmen, complimented the lush green gardens in front. Arched windows, set in iron casings, ornamented each tower and structure. Even the patches of ivy and moss added appeal. The scene was a dream—charming and elegant, yet distinguished and noble.

"I have it on good authority the duke and his family dine here regularly, though I do not understand why. The house is shabby at best." Aunt Prudence ran her gloves down the front of her skirts. "Grant Estate is far superior, in more ways than one. I never favored Mrs. Ainsworth. She was always trying to best everyone at the pianoforte and cards."

Rose bit her cheek. Her aunt's complaints would not diminish her excitement; nothing could. Musicales were as common occurrences as dinner parties, but Rose had yet to be permitted to attend either. She had long imagined the joy of listening to a room full of friends sharing in music. She had the smallest inkling that something in her life was about to change, if only she could persevere her aunt. She allowed a smile to pass over her lips. "You look well, Aunt."

Prudence's frown twisted into a pucker. "Posh. You know nothing of what looks well or not. Now, remember, keep quiet unless spoken to. Understand?"

The footmen opened the carriage door, escorting both women to the stone path.

Rose was grateful for the strength of solid ground. Voices emanated from the open doors. She strained her ears, searching for one particular voice.

"Mrs. Prudence Grant and her niece, Miss Grant," Prudence said to the butler at the entry threshold.

The man was tall and slender, and his gray eyes were rather deep set. His lips settled in a straight line. "This way, Mrs. Grant, Miss Grant," he said, leading them through the domed entry and into the reception hall.

Rose's eyes studied the curve of the stone and the stain glass at the far end of the room. Prudence's description of the Milton Manor as shabby could not have been further from the truth. Rose's slippers slid across the stones—each one worn away by the footprints of those that had gone before. She imagined the house had enough history to fill volumes in the library.

Clusters of people stood along the walls and corners of the open room. The candle chandelier was adorned with crystals, and was lit to its exquisite magnificence, sending splinters of light all across the area.

Rose's eyes flickered across the party, until they landed upon Colin. He stood on the far end of the room, conversing with a group of women. She took a shaky breath, clasping her hands together. He wore a dark coat with light blue trousers. His brown waves had been miraculously tamed. Even with his masked expression, he was handsome.

"Mrs. Grant and her niece, Miss Grant," the butler announced to the crowd.

Conversation fell to silence as the assembled guests turned toward the pair of women. Rose curtsied, bowing her head, and lifted her gaze to the onlooking faces. Curiosity shone from all directions.

"Mrs. Grant, Miss Grant," the hostess, Miss Ainsworth, said, curtsying in reply. Her silver hair was pinned with precision underneath a large and feathery headpiece. Her honey brown eyes were warm, and she took Rose's hand. "When the marquess suggested we extend an invitation, I was overjoyed. It's been too long since I have chanced to see you, dear."

Rose grasped Mrs. Ainsworth's hand and tried to ignore the pinching of the corset. "Yes, decidedly too long, Mrs. Ainsworth."

The hostess was another of Rose's mother's friends. Mrs. Ainsworth and Rose had met periodically throughout the years—a chance meeting on a rare shopping trip or momentary glances from across the Sunday service—but Prudence had never allowed Rose extensive time to visit.

Prudence cleared her throat. "Adriana."

Mrs. Ainsworth sighed. "Prudence, do come in. I would be glad to make any necessary introductions."

Prudence sneered. Her brows pulled into sharp arches. "I

am quite acquainted with the social circles of Andover and London, Adriana, but thank you all the same."

"Rose?" Mrs. Ainsworth asked, flicking her head to a group of women behind her. "Will you allow me?"

Rose's mouth turned dry. Since her governess had left three years prior, Rose had little opportunity for socializing. Despite Rose's desire to cultivate friendships, a nervousness fluttered inside her stomach. "Thank you. I would be much obliged."

Like a heavy curtain, the women descended upon Rose, blocking all view of the marquess. The ladies curtsied and offered "how do you do's". They admired her dress and hair. One woman even asked for the name of her lady's maid. Rose hardly knew how to answer the questions—they came at a startling speed and variety.

When at last the curtain parted and Rose met the glance of Colin, relief—like a warm fire on a cold evening—settled over her trembling limbs. His masked expression softened, and his ever-changing colored eyes—emerald in the candlelight—swept over her with notable consideration.

Her pulse quickened to a startling degree.

"And will you be favoring us with a musical selection, Miss Grant?"

She flinched, turning at the sound of the voice. A pair of light eyes peered at her with marked attention. There was something strikingly familiar about those eyes; in fact, Rose had just witnessed their likeness in the marquess only a moment earlier. Rose studied the woman's dress, made from what appeared to be imported silk and trimmings. Only one woman at this party could emit such effortless dignity. "Yes, Your Grace."

Mrs. Ainsworth smiled. "Forgive me, Duchess. I failed to introduce you to the new addition—Miss Rose Grant, granddaughter of the Honorable Lord Josiah Grant. Rose, meet my dear friend, the Honorable Duchess of Andover."

"Yes, I hear I have you to thank for the return of my husband, Miss Grant," the duchess said with a slight smile. Her cheeks were a lovely shade of pink, and her soft voice put Rose's worries at ease. "Thank you."

"I was happy to assist the duke, Your Grace." Rose's gaze flickered toward the marquess. She could sense the weight of Colin's watch. "And will you be participating tonight?"

The duchess dipped her chin in affirmation. "Adriana insists, and so I have brought my violin."

Mrs. Ainsworth beamed, linking her arm in Rose's. "Speaking of music, I do believe the appointed time has come. Rose, you must sit between me and the duchess. I insist."

"I would be glad to." Rose looked at Prudence, wishing for the warmth and familiarity that was expected of an aunt. Yet, there was no such feeling around Prudence. Rose was more inclined to sit between an acquaintance and stranger.

The windows of the music room faced the setting sun, brightening the already vivid tapestries and portraits lining the long and narrow space. Open doors led to an adjoining balcony. Rose peered out the nearest one, inhaling the fresh air.

She had always supposed Grant Estate to be perfectly situated. The lands were impressive—yes. But what if Rose's attachment to her childhood home persisted simply because she had not been to other places? Milton Manor was certainly challenging her adoration for her home; how many other places might?

The party situated themselves amongst the sofas and chairs, all directed at the pianoforte.

Aunt Prudence scowled at Rose from across the room. She was seated by Mr. Higgins.

Suddenly, the corset felt indisputably tighter. Rose inhaled, setting her hands against her middle. Was the glare of her aunt enough to undo her in such a ridiculous way? Her breath turned shallow, and she felt her chest spasm from the efforts.

"Rose, are you well?" Mrs. Ainsworth asked, clasping her hand.

Rose looked to her aunt for comfort. Surely she must sense her discomfort.

Prudence fanned herself with a hand, returning Rose's questioning glance with a smirk. Rose blinked furiously. Surely she had imagined the disdain of her aunt. Surely Prudence was not so unfeeling.

Rose gasped once more. The corset tightened again with the effort, nearly crushing her lungs.

"Miss Grant?" the duchess asked, leaning closer. "You look unwell. May I assist you in some way?"

Rose clutched the hand of the duchess and whispered, but desperation dripped from her words. "My corset. I cannot breathe."

The duchess stood instantly, alongside Mrs. Ainsworth, and the pair of them whisked Rose from the room. She clung to their arms, moving her legs as quickly as she could. However, fear grasped at her, trembling in her legs and spreading to her arms.

Mrs. Ainsworth ushered Rose into an adjoining room and closed the door. The hostess, along with the duchess, loosed the back of Rose's dress without a single word, ripping apart the laced and tortuous contraption.

With a snap, the undergarment fell to the floor. Rose crumpled down with it, spasming in relief. Warm tears rolled down her cheeks. Death had felt certain a moment ago.

The duchess crouched beside her, stroking her wet cheeks. "There, you are free."

Mrs. Ainsworth picked up the pieces of ribbing, studying them carefully. Her cheerful demeanor had darkened considerably, and she pulled at laces, turning them over in her hand. "Who did this to you?"

Rose winced, burying her face in her hands. Prudence's smirk flashed in her mind once more, and Rose shook her head in denial. Her voice cracked in emotion, "My aunt requested I wear the garment. She worried about my form and posture. I am sure she never thought to injure me."

Mrs. Ainsworth exchanged glances with the duchess. After a full minute of silence, the hostess sighed. "My darling Rose, I have failed you."

Rose shook her head. "Whatever do you mean? You have always been kind and good to me."

Mrs. Ainsworth frowned, and emotion glistened in her eyes. "Your mother would not have stood for such treatment. Do you have any idea what this contraption is?"

"A corset."

"Yes, but an ancient and terribly tortuous one—a corset meant to be worn for only short moments of time, as the ribbing contracts with each movement. If we had not removed it in such a fashion, you might not be alive." Mrs. Ainsworth clasped her hands so tightly that her fingers ran white. "Your aunt would have known."

"No." Rose shook her head, rising to her feet. She pulled her dress sleeves over her shoulders and drew in a sharp breath. "That is impossible. Aunt Prudence helped to raise me. She is not capable of such cruelty."

The duchess took Rose's hand. "Let us do up your dress, dear. We will return to the musicale as if nothing has happened. Not a word of this incident. Tomorrow, I will send this contraption to an investigator and see what he can discover."

Rose wiped at her eyes. She wanted to believe the entire

ordeal was a misunderstanding, a disastrous mistake. But a smirking Prudence once more flashed across her memory. Rose pushed away the nudging sensation in her gut. *No.* Prudence was disapproving and harsh—at times, irrefutably cold. But wishing to cause Rose harm at her first social outing? The idea was preposterous. She could not believe it —she would not.

Her insides coiled, and a chill ran down her spine as she looked at the remnants of the corset. A simple truth shone back at her, as clearly as a reflection. Her aunt's disdain for her ran far deeper than jealousy or irritation; Aunt Prudence despised Rose.

* * *

COLIN PACED THE ROOM, peering onto the balcony. The sun was just setting; red, purples, and oranges flared across the sky.

Being around Rose again only confirmed his suspicions; he wished to know her better, and standing in the back of the music room offered him the best view of her, without appearing too obvious. Only...where had she gone? Colin turned his back for a brief moment to converse with a Mr. Higgins, and Rose had disappeared—as had his mother and Mrs. Ainsworth.

Colin tried to distract his thoughts. He studied the clouds —wisps against the colorful canvas, patches of blue and white amidst the brilliancy. Had the world always presented such beauty—sunsets the colors of fairytales?

"Lord Stratfordshire," Mr. Higgins said, standing uncomfortably near. His breath reeked of garlic and onion. The man was a known hermit, and gossip stated he only ventured into society at the command of Rose's aunt. "Tell me, do you think the summer will be dry?"

Colin clasped his hands behind his back. There were few things that tired the marquess more than small talk, especially that of the weather. Yet, his upbringing inclined him to humor the stranger. He offered a nod. "I believe rain has come near every afternoon this week. Has it not? Is that not a good start, Mr. Higgins?"

"Exactly what I told Mrs. Grant." Mr. Higgins wiped his nose, flicking his thumb around a spot near his left nostril for a disturbingly long moment. He wheezed, combing his thin gray hair many times over. "And what of gaming at Andover? Have your pheasants cultivated enough offspring?"

The marquess's mouth dropped in surprise; he had never been asked about pheasant offspring. Hunting was a common enough topic, but Colin did not know how best to reply. He had never kept tabs on the hatchlings near Stratforshire.

A door opened from across the room, and Mrs. Ainsworth clapped her hands. "Please forgive the delay."

Colin's eyes wandered behind the hostess.

Rose stood at his mother's side. Her hazel eyes glistened, and lines of worry scattered her expression. Colin's mother gripped Rose's arm. The duchess's light eyes were wrinkled near the edges, and her lips twisted into a pucker.

Colin shifted his weight. His mother's anger, though imperceptible to most, was unmistakable; her wrath only kindled on limited occasions, and Colin recognized the expression. The duchess did not upset easily. Her few occasions of fury were sparked by earnest concerns. First and foremost, the duchess was a mother. She was instinctively protective. From his experience nearly breaking his back falling from the roof as a child, or the time a nurse had raised a voice needlessly, he knew what anger looked like on his mother's features and he saw it now.

Colin gulped. What on earth could have transpired between the three women?

"Now, we will proceed with the program, beginning with a vocal selection by Miss Anna Porter and accompanied by her sister, Miss Eliza." Mrs. Ainsworth resumed her position on the sofa.

Rose trembled, and a single tear slipped down her cheek.

The duchess lifted a hand to Mrs. Ainsworth shoulder and leaned in. Colin strained his ears to hear her. "But first— I am afraid Miss Grant has suffered a terrible headache. I will send her home in my carriage. Please carry on with the program. I will return momentarily."

Prudence sighed. "Already? I would have thought you might last longer, child." She turned, and her lips smacked together. Her whisper carried well across the room. "Poor dear has the constitution of a kitten."

Colin gritted his teeth, watching Prudence in disbelief. She did not rise to meet her niece; she did not even protest Rose's departure. The woman was unfeeling and, worse, contented to humiliate her niece in a time of discomfort.

Colin hurried across the room, offering his arm to Rose.

Her tear-filled eyes lifted, and her lips parted. "Thank you, Lord Stratfordshire."

"I am sorry for your headache." Colin felt useless. He doubted Rose had a headache at all, and if she did, it was the result of something far heavier. "Will you allow me to help you to the carriage?"

Rose sniffled, dipping her chin.

The duchess stroked a gloved hand across Colin's shoulder. "Yes, please escort her, Colin. I will have Mrs. Ainsworth's footman retrieve our carriage this instant."

"Come, this way, Miss Grant," he said, leading her back through the reception hall and into the foyer. The rooms, filled with liveliness and laughter only moments ago, were now silent. Their footsteps echoed along the stone steps and floors. "I know it is not my place to ask—"

A single sob split between her lips. She shook her head, but her voice remained shaky. "Please, Lord Stratfordshire. You are kind to inquire, but it is only a headache."

Colin turned, facing her fully. Her watery glance seemed to plead; she did not wish him to press her further. Her distress was too fresh. Colin placed a hand over her fingers that rested on his other arm. "I am sorry to see you go, Miss Grant."

Her lips curved, and another set of tears slipped down in response. "Thank you. I look forward to seeing you again, hopefully before too much time has passed. If ever you are near Grant Estate, do stop by."

"I would be glad to." Colin inwardly cringed. He sounded so stiff, so formal. "That is—I shall call on you in the coming week."

She wiped at her tears.

Colin startled, reaching for his handkerchief. "Here, do take this."

"But I could not—"

"Please." He locked eyes with her. The tears had changed her hazel eyes to a deep green. Colin's heart thudded against his chest. He longed to understand her, more than he had wished to understand anyone. The intensity of his desire surprised him. What was it about Rose that affected him so fully?

She accepted the handkerchief. "Thank you."

He took in a slow breath, surveying her serious expression.

"Miss Grant," the duchess said, bursting through the reception hall. "As I said, not a word about"—her stare landed on Colin—"the carriage."

Colin's brows furrowed, and he widened his stance. His

mother had never been a skilled liar. "The carriage? Not a word about the carriage?"

Rose retreated a few steps, curtsying to the duchess. "Your Grace, I shall not mention your generosity to a soul."

The duchess managed a smile. "Now, Colin, you must return to the music room. The program has started, and I wish to have a final word with Miss Grant...about her dreadful headache."

He bowed and left, determined to uncover whatever atrocity had befallen Rose.

CHAPTER 6

*A*fter morning light entered her room, and despite her attempts to fall back asleep, Rose laid in bed, staring at the red-bellied bullfinch perched upon the ledge of her window. His song—soft and broken, yet unfailingly beautiful—ignited an ache in her chest. She had always considered herself like the finches, at times small and insignificant but forever cheerful and contented.

Her rosy image of the world had been shattered at the musicale the previous night. Aunt Prudence had cast her net about Rose, determined to humiliate her and bring her song to silence. That, or end her existence altogether.

Rose was grateful when she did not see her aunt at the breakfast table. Her grandfather, however, was in one of his difficult moods.

Lord Josiah Grant was not a man to be trifled with. He cared for a breakfast of poached eggs and buttered toast—not a thing more. He pushed his plate forward, and he tapped his fingers on the table. "Mrs. Blackburn. Where is she? I distinctly told her I did not wish for plum pudding. Where is my usual spread?"

Rose stood from the table in response. Her appetite had been scarce to begin with but had fled the instant her grandfather had begun spouting off complaints.

The day had only begun, but her eyes were swollen and red from a night of tears. Worse, her head pounded with each tinkling of her fork against the china. "I will find her and ask her to bring you your usual, Grandfather."

He let out a puff of air, pushing his tongue into the side of his wrinkled cheek. "Tell her I will not stand for such disobedience."

"As you wish," she said, stalking toward the kitchen.

She took a shaky breath and leaned against the archway of the kitchen. Her grandfather's mood only discouraged her further. Was there no happiness to be found at Grant Estate? Was Rose bound to a life of misery, locked between a miserable man and a frightful aunt?

"Mrs. Blackburn." Scolding anyone, let along those that lived to serve the Grant family, seemed wrong. She could not do such a thing, especially to Mrs. Blackburn. The cook hadn't a mean bone in her body.

Mrs. Blackburn turned her head. "Miss Grant, how are you this morning? Off to the gardens already?"

Rose surveyed the open door and the flood of light. Motes sparkled across the rays. "My grandfather—"

"The plum pudding." The statement came with a soft sigh. The cook shook her head and dusted her hands together. She took up a spoon and began mixing a bowlful of flour and spices. "I knew he would be bothered by the gesture."

Rose swallowed. "Then why did you persist in going against his wishes? His nerves wind tighter and tighter. Please do not test him, Mrs. Blackburn."

The woman dropped a wooden spoon to the counter. "The chickens—seems a dog got into the eggs again. I had only enough for the pudding, and I hoped he would not mind the change for once. Plum pudding was his favorite, at least before the accident."

"I see." Rose crossed her arms, rubbing her hands against her suddenly chilled arms.

Mrs. Blackburn nodded. "I will speak to him straight away, Miss…" She paused, meeting Rose's eyes. The cook frowned, and her voice turned gentle. "Rose, what has happened? You look as if you've had a row. Has your aunt been plucking away at you again?"

The weight that Rose had tried so hard to discard settled once more against her chest, pressing harder and harder against her sluggish heartbeat. She shook her head, albeit much to hesitantly to be considered convincing. "No. I am only tired." *Tired of trying to please my aunt and grandfather. Tired of singing a song that no one else understands.*

"Then you still have a headache?"

Rose bit her bottom lip. Hours of crying did make for a slicing ache. "Yes, quite."

Mrs. Blackburn opened a cupboard and retrieved a tincture. "My mother used to give me this whenever I had such a malady. Take a swallow as needed."

"Thank you." Rose pressed the bottle to her chest and smiled. There was still kindness in the world, despite the difficulties ahead. The beam of light from the open door lengthened, warming the front of her. "Perhaps I shall take that walk after all, Mrs. Blackburn."

"Take care, Miss Grant."

Rose meandered through the kitchen garden, stopping at the well. She wished for a carefree afternoon with her mother and the opportunity to hear her mother's laughter once again. The memory, usually one of happiness and comfort, only deepened the ache within her ribcage, and Rose forged onward along the path she had ridden with the marquess. She paused at the pond and creeks, the towering oaks and path along the duke's lands.

But each beloved place seemed unexpectedly hollow, meaningless.

Jealousy plagued Prudence—and why shouldn't it? Rose's father had been a clear favorite of the family, in terms of inheritance and general respectability, and now, Rose's grandfather still preferred Rose over Prudence.

As if the unfairness was not enough, Aunt Prudence remained unattached and in her forties. Shamed by a duke, rejected by London society despite her noble upbringing— bitterness seemed an expected result.

Rose closed her eyes, holding back emotion. For so long, Rose had made exceptions for Prudence, reasoning away her aunt's dark heart and obvious slights. Perhaps that was the most tragic bit of the situation—Rose's wasted effort, her needless attempts at winning Prudence's affection.

Footsteps padded through the dry grass, stopping only feet away from where she sat. "Rose?"

She looked up at the young man standing above her. A ribbon of relief threaded through her pain. "Paul Garvey, how ever did you find me?"

He sat in the grass beside her. His dark eyes seemed almost as empty as Rose felt. "I had to, and so I followed the sounds of your sobbing."

"My sobs...?" Her eyes widened, and she ran her fingers over her moistened cheeks. She had not noticed the tears nor her whimpering. She lifted her cuffs to her eyes, wiping furiously. "I had not realized..."

Paul pressed his lips together. "I've come to speak with you about your aunt."

She winced. He could not possibly know about the corset. "What about her?"

He tapped at her arm, commanding her gaze to his. "Rose,

I've just had word about her plans for you. I had to tell you. Something must be done. My father is friends with her driver. Apparently, the driver overheard her discussing something with Mr. Higgins."

"I've already found out about the corset, Paul. You do not need to warn me."

"The corset?" His eyes held more questions than answers, and a line near the center of his brows deepened. "I know nothing of that. I am speaking of Mr. Higgins and the marquess."

Rose stood, turning away from him. Self-preservation kept her from fleeing but facing him straight on felt near impossible after her scare the previous evening. "Tell me quickly."

He took a moment, seeming to collect his thoughts. Then he stood, stepping directly behind her. "She means to ruin you, Rose—with the help of Mr. Higgins. Your aunt seems to think you've caught the eye of the marquess and future Duke of Andover. She means to have Mr. Higgins compromise you in order to prevent such a union."

In order to prevent such a union. The absurdity of the assumption rattled Rose's anger. Lord Stratfordshire had been warm, perhaps even expressed interest in furthering his acquaintance with her. But why did Prudence have to jump to such a conclusion? And how could Prudence seek to destroy Rose's reputation and foreseeable future? How could anyone think of such an abominable scheme?

Rose spun on her heels. Heat blossomed in her chest. "Paul, are you sure of this? When does she mean to enact this plan?"

"My father did not say, but he sent me to warn you." He shifted his weight, and his voice lowered. "I worried you would not believe me. You have always seen the good in Prudence, much more than anyone else could."

Her lips trembled, and she shook her head. "No, I was as blind as my grandfather. I refused to see the truth. I followed her every direction, but Paul, I am no longer blind. I am painfully—so very, very painfully—aware of her designs now. She is evil, and I cannot stay here any longer. Grant Estate no longer holds the promise of happiness, no matter how I hope or try to wish it."

Paul folded his arms. "I do not know whether to mourn that you are leaving or cheer you on in your escape. Perhaps I may do both?"

She collapsed in his arms. "You've been my dearest friend. I will miss you."

"Where will you go?" he asked, pulling away to look at her. "You have no relations in London. You cannot take up employment."

Rose swallowed. "I have an aunt in Andover. I will leave tonight, if you will help me."

Paul's eyes widened. "Then you must pack, straight away. Meet me in the kitchen gardens after midnight, and I will have a wagon waiting."

She spun around the open field, taking in each rock and tufted mound. She would miss this place, if only for the memories it had given way to.

Despite what she had previously imagined to be true, recollections were not embedded in trees or wishing wells or halls where laughter once rung; they were more than fields of flowers or portraits hanging by her grandfather's door. Sentiments were more than flashes of faces and infinitely more powerful than time and separation.

Rose clutched at her chest. She would take them all—the good and the bad, the joy and the pain—but she would not turn back. There was only one thing left to do, and so Rose hurried to the corner bedroom at the top of the stairs.

As always, she stopped a few feet short of the door. *Her*

mother's portrait. Tears built behind her eyes. Rose traced her mother's features until each slant and curve of her mother's face etched into her memory; she would carry the picture with her.

"Rose, is that you?" her grandfather asked from the other side of the cracked door.

He always sensed her nearness before she entered the room, and though her grandfather's treatment seemed to sway as drastically as his moods, Lord Grant was as close to a father as Rose had known. His loving touch and soft words were, after her mother's passing, all she saw of familial love.

"Yes, I have come to see you." Rose wiped at her eyes, glancing once more at her mother's face. "If that is conducive to your schedule?"

He sat in a chair near the window, pressing his wrinkly fingers to the glass. He turned his head toward her voice, but his eyes were clouded, aimless. "I suppose I may be able to pencil you in, granddaughter."

Rose halted, and her recently repressed tears threatened once more. How appropriate it was that she find him in good spirits before her parting. She sat in an opposite chair and looked down below. "Shall I describe the view then?"

"Mmm, yes. I have been picturing the absurd—wild turkeys running about, the gardeners' neglect, and my daughter scolding the lot of them, turkeys included." Lord Grant chuckled at his own amusement. He leaned his forehead to the window. "I can feel the warmth though."

Rose cleared her throat, hoping to disguise her emotion. "Not a turkey to be seen, Grandfather. Further, the gardeners are hard at work. If you'll strain, you can hear the—"

"Clipping of the hedge sheers."

She swallowed and placed a hand to his knee. "Exactly so. The roses are blooming, and I found such a pretty patch of wildflowers on my walk yesterday. I could have sat in the field for hours, smelling them. My mother would have." Her voice cracked on the word 'mother'. Rose hung her head.

Lord Grant remained silent, but he gripped her hand and reached his other to touch her face. "Ah, just what I imagined —wet with tears. You are not one to cry, my dear. What has happened?"

She had already contemplated, but ultimately decided against, telling him about the corset. Instead, she brought his other hand to her cheeks, falling on her knees before him. "I have something I must tell you, and I hope you will understand."

"You are leaving me."

She gasped, shaking under his touch. "I do not wish to leave you, but I must. I cannot stay here any longer."

He sighed, running a thumb along her jaw. "I knew this day would come. Prudence already keeps you under lock and key. A young woman should not be so confined and controlled. I've often thought to challenge her, but my feebleness, as much as my own despondence, has kept me from doing so. Her jealousies have taken their toll. Where will you go?"

Questions swam at her. She had not expected his apology nor his quick understanding. "Then you are not angry with me?"

He dropped his hands from her face, returning them to the warmth of the glass. His lips pulled into a frown. "I am not angry, but I must know. Where will you go?"

"My mother's sister in Andover. I leave tonight, but I beg you will not tell Prudence. She will wish me back, wish to remind me of her power…"

He faced her directly, and his aimless glance held tears. "I would not breathe a word for all the world."

Rose fell into his embrace, where they cried together. "I will come back for you, once my life is sorted."

He kissed her cheek. "I will pray you sort things quickly then."

* * *

COLIN CRINKLED THE PAPER, reading the lines once more before balling it into a wad and tossing it across the room.

Dear Miss Grant,

I regretted your absence at the musical three days ago. My mother assures me your headache was severe but that I am not to worry. She seems to think I am like the rest of the party—blind and gullible. I have done little else but worry on your account. Are you well and recovered from what truly ailed you?

Your departure from Milton Manor was followed by another disastrous turn of events. My mother seemed to misplace something of enormous importance, as far as sentimentality goes. Mrs. Ainsworth ordered her staff to search the entirety of the house but with little success. It seems your departure was poor luck. I am inclined to believe the opposite as well.

May I call on you in two days?

Lord Stratfordshire

The ticking of the clock sliced through the silent and stiff study. The shelves upon shelves were each meticulously clean and ordered. The desk was stained and polished regularly, without a single scratch nor divot.

Colin pressed his fingers to his temples, massaging them. He felt altogether too much like the room. He maintained appearances with precision, and as a result, he was turning out to be a rather stiff character. Yet, both times he had been near Rose, Colin had felt awakened—alive.

Why did she have to leave? And right before the loss of his mother's heirloom? The coupling of events left for a difficult evening indeed.

He took up the second letter, the one that had been sent along with his returned letter.

Dearest Lord Stratfordshire,

I regret to inform you of my niece's departure. Miss Grant has left Grant Estate for an undeterminable amount of time. She left with little notice, and with even less attention to me and her grandfather, Lord Josiah Grant. Consequently, I am returning your letter. I felt it my duty, and I hope you will forgive her impudence and offense.

Sincerely,

Mrs. Prudence Grant

Colin knocked his knuckles against the edge of the paper. His mother had refused to indulge his curiosity and inquiries concerning the musicale and Rose. And now, Rose was gone.

A knock sounded at the door.

"Yes?" Colin asked, sliding the letter inside his top drawer.

The duchess peeked in the room. She was wearing her new bonnet, and she carried a basket of fresh rolls. "Colin, I hoped you would wish to accompany me. I thought to send along a treat to the Smith family. Their little boy seems well on his way to recovering."

Colin stood, and his lips tugged. Seeing his mother made repressing a smile near impossible. She was a lovely woman, with an even greater heart, which was why her refusal to speak of the musicale was all the stranger. "I wish I could, Mother, but I am afraid I have something pressing to attend to."

She frowned. "If you must, but please, Colin. You need to stop brooding. You will see her again."

He lifted a brow. "Pardon?"

The duchess set the basket on his desk, and the pleasant aroma of fresh bread filled the room. She tugged on the edge of her lace gloves. "I speak of Miss Grant, of course. You are quite smitten with her, but Colin, I must warn you. There is more to her than…I mean to say, if you were to entangle yourself with her, I am afraid you might put yourself very much in danger."

Irritation pricked the back of his neck. "Mother, are you asking me to let her go?"

She held his glance, and she combed over his expression with marked caution. "No, but I am asking you to take care. Miss Grant comes with other alliances—alliances you would do well to consider."

He blinked. "Are you speaking of her aunt?"

"Yes."

"Then you are of the opinion that Rose may share in some of Mrs. Prudence Grant's character?" Colin had already read through letter after letter detailing Prudence's long list of offenses. After his request to invite Rose to the musicale, it seemed multiple attendees thought it their duty to alert the marquess of Prudence's shortcomings.

At one time, decades before, Prudence had been the talk of all London. Her father's title, along with the fortune, made for a respectable match. Even more compelling, according to the sources, was Prudence's beauty. In her prime, London could not provide an equal. With no rivals in terms of status and allure, many believed her to be in the running as the future duchess—in the very place Colin's mother now sat. Colin shuddered at the thought.

"No, I do not worry on that account," the duchess said, sinking to the Grecian couch. She sighed, leaning against the side rest. "Miss Grant favors her mother."

Colin's throat turned dry. The downward spiral to Prudence's character had begun with Lillian Parson. When Colin's father began pursuing Lillian, Prudence transformed into quite the scheming and jealous woman—spreading hateful lies, paying servants to ruin Miss Parson's gowns, and, on at least one occasion, even attempted to poison the dressmaker's daughter. Nothing was ever proved, but rumors took flight.

Prudence's chances at marriage were ruined altogether— and Miss Parson? She had rejected Colin's father, falling for the very brother of the woman that had tried to hurt her.

Colin moved to the front of the desk and leaned against it. "Did you dislike Rose's mother?"

The duchess's eyelids lowered, and a strange expression— part humor, pity, and humiliation—overtook her feminine features. "I should be grateful to Lillian. She broke your father's heart, and he was in desperate need of mending. I was glad to take up the role, seeing how I loved him already…"

"You said you should be grateful to her, but you are not?" Colin leaned closer, reaching for her hand.

She shook her head. "Your father loves me with all the tenderness I could ask for. He is kind and good and unfailingly cheerful. Yet… I have sensed on more than one occasion a melancholy in him—a longing in a moment of silence, a brokenness that I thought had been mended."

There was no disagreeing with his mother; Colin had sensed similar qualities in his father. Colin well imagined his mother's pain. "Then you think he never stopped loving her?"

"Nothing so tragic, son. Your father is faithful and honest. He loves me with every part of himself. It is only… I often wonder—was it the loss of Miss Parson that caused so much pain, or was it more? I think he lost a large part of himself with her departure, a part he has never been able to regain. I never understood such a thing, until I met Miss Grant."

Colin cleared his throat. "What do you mean?"

"You have come alive since you met her, as if your soul has lay in wait for your entire twenty-five years to find her."

His cheeks flushed. How had his mother supposed what he was just coming to suspect?

She squeezed his hand. "Do not worry. I shall not whisper a word."

Colin gasped, laughing in surprise. "If you have already surmised as much, I imagine others might not be far behind. I shall have to school my manners better."

"No, Colin." The duchess straightened and stood, still holding his hand. Her eyes glistened with seeming emotion. "Do not lose this new part of yourself, or you may never find it again. Take caution, but do not surrender to the likes of Mrs. Prudence Grant or anyone else. You will live to regret such a thing."

He handed his mother the basket. "What makes you so sure Miss Grant will have me in return?"

The duchess rolled her eyes, and her lips flinched. "Colin, when you look at her the way you do, you are quite impossible to resist."

"But she is gone from Hampshire, at least by her aunt's account."

The duchess turned, stopping at the door of the study. She glanced over her shoulder, and mischief gleamed in her stare. "Then you will have to find her."

CHAPTER 7

ndover, England
July 1814

The white linen blew across the clothes line, acting as clouds against the blue sky. Rose walked the length of the fluttering fabric, pausing near the end. Rolling fields and winding roads stretched for miles. The wind carried with it a waft of the nearby flower garden. Scented stocks were a favorite of the duke, according to her cousin Oliver.

Rose had never imagined loving a place as much as her childhood home. However, six weeks under Amelia's roof had changed her perception drastically. There were things more important than furnishings and drawing rooms, things more imperative than expansive lands and refined taste. A smile touched her lips as softly as the breeze.

"Come in before you catch a sunburn, my dear," Amelia called from the front doorway. Her aunt stood a few inches shorter than her, and her black locks were fashioned into one long braid that hung over a shoulder. "I've warmed some tea. Come, take some refreshment."

Rose laughed, pulling up the bonnet that hung from her

neck. Some things did not change, but the reasons did. She did her best to obey Amelia—much like she had Prudence—but now, Rose did so happily. She strode up the rock path, stopping to admire the cottage.

Her aunt's home was less than a tenth the size of Grant Estate. Built in the English Tudor style, replete with a thatched roof, the house only reached two stories high. There were three bedrooms total, with only a small kitchen and dining room and one cozy parlor. Yet, the home held more sunshine and laughter than her grandfather's estate ever had.

"I had hoped for a walk today. I haven't been to see Oliver at work for nearly a week. He is so grateful for the picnics I pack," Rose said, climbing the front step.

Oliver worked the duke's gardens, particularly the apple orchard which had quickly become one of Rose's favorite places. There was something comforting about the rows of trees and the scent of apples. The shade seemed made for walking and contemplation, and Rose had plenty to consider. She had left Prudence without a letter. Self-preservation battled that guilt, and Rose did not know which would win in the end.

Amelia waved her inside. "I see no harm in your walks, so long as you take your bonnet. A sunburn is not to be endured on such a lovely complexion."

Rose smiled and walked into the front room. "I will take care to protect it then, Aunt."

"I am glad to hear." Amelia poured the tea, and her fragile frame shook. "Your mother would have scoffed at such a directive. She was much like you, always wishing to traipse about the country. I suppose that is where you first learned to love the outdoors."

Rose took the first cup of tea, holding it between both hands. The tea swirled in a circle. Amelia spoke so often about Rose's mother. With each warm recollection, Rose somehow felt nearer to her mother. Each detail of Amelia's memories seemed to restore a portion of Rose's mother's character; the puzzle was beginning to take shape after only a month and a half.

Her aunt cleared her throat and set a tea biscuit on her plate. "You still have not asked about the duke and his family. I would have thought you would be curious, particularly in the case of the marquess. The future duke is a truly handsome man." Amelia sat on the sofa, the furniture creaking beneath her slight weight. She adjusted the teacups and saucers on the front table. The dishes clinked together, tinkling in a musical way. Her full lips pulled into a smile. "If I were young and beautiful such as you, I might *wish* to run into the marquess in the gardens."

Rose laughed, sitting next to her aunt. She had not found a way to tell her cousins and aunt that she was already acquainted with the duke and family. "The way you said that almost sounded as if you wish me to meet Lord Stratfordshire."

"He is highly eligible, and from what the other servants tell Oliver, Lord Stratfordshire is said to be in an especially brooding mood after his recent trip to his tenant lands."

"Oh?" Rose took a sweet from the tray.

Amelia, apparently brimming with eagerness, set her cup to the table. Her dark eyes beamed, and her dimples appeared. "Yes. I have heard he met a young lady there, only briefly, but evidently long enough to make an impression. He has been writing contacts all over the county and even London in hopes of discovering her whereabouts. Seems the lady's guardians were unwilling to divulge the information. Can you imagine? If I had a daughter and Lord Stratfordshire was to pursue her, I would gladly accept the attentions. No lady could do better."

"You say he is actively searching her out?" Rose's mind spun. She had thought of Colin many times, especially of their last meeting at the musicale. He had shown her the utmost kindness. She often held his handkerchief and contemplated the way he had inquired about her well-being. "Are you sure?"

"Quite."

Rose took another sip of her tea. She had wished to see him, but since her arrival at the cottage, Rose had focused on becoming acquainted with her aunt and cousins instead.

Amelia closed her eyes. "This tea. Since your arrival, we have eaten like the duke himself. However did you think to pack such niceties for us? The flour and spices were particularly needed, but the tea and tins of sweets... Thank you, Rose."

"I felt horrible for the way I came—in the thick of night." A tremor ran down Rose's back. The clouds had blanketed the moon that night, and Paul had nearly crashed the wagon twice in the darkness.

"We were happy to receive you, day or night. Besides, after what you've been through with Prudence, I suspect there was no other way." Amelia squinted, staring out the window. Sunlight poured into the room, but Rose could just make out the figure of her two younger cousins. "Seems the boys are back already."

"Perhaps they had success at the fishing pond?" Rose asked, standing.

The twins' laughter grew louder as they thumped up the steps. They were fifteen, at the cusp of manhood, yet clinging to their carefree and childish ways.

Amelia opened the door to a soppy sight. Her hands flew to her hips. "What on earth?"

Simon lifted a line of fish in the air. His black curls clung to his forehead, and a line of pond residue was strewn across his right shoulder. "I've bested Eli in a matter of an hour, Mother, and so he sent me into the pond."

Eli twisted his mouth into a frown, settling his hands at his side. Rose bit back a smile. At least he attempted at regret, though mischief flitted across his crinkled brows. "I'm prepared for my scolding, but I think it a very poor sport that will not offer advice to a laboring fisherman."

"Is that so?" Amelia poked a finger into Simon's dripping shirt. Her breath turned raspy, and a new set of lines appeared beside her eyes. "Oh, boys. I cannot keep up with the messes you make. Simon, take off your shirt and shoes outside. I'll have to do another batch of laundry, even though Rose already spent the morning laboring at the task."

Rose peeked her head around Amelia. "I do not mind taking the task, Aunt, and afterward, perhaps I will take that walk we spoke of."

Eli swallowed hard, his Adam's apple bobbing up and down. "I didn't mean to cause you more trouble, Rose. I only wished to teach Simon a thing or two."

"Ha," Amelia said, pulling him by the ear. "I imagine this shall teach you a thing or two. Now, put the fish near the hearth. You will take the axe from the back door. There is wood to be chopped, especially if we are to fry the fish."

Simon lifted his chin, and Rose recognized the look of satisfaction. "Just as I told him, Mother."

Amelia's brows rose. "You will join him."

Simon protested, throwing his hands in the air. "But Mother—"

"But nothing."

The second boy tore off the sopping wet shirt and dropped it to the ground. His satisfaction melted into visible annoyance.

Rose felt a familiar stab at the back of her throat. Seeing her cousins interact with their mother always brought a longing. Even their bickering was endearing—nothing like the moments Rose had shared with Prudence. For with every exchange, Amelia's love was written in her caring eyes, her adoring gaze, her dimples manifested across her pinched cheeks. Certainly Amelia angered at times, even yelled on occasion, but her love was always there, shining beneath each scolding like the sunlight pouring through the window.

Rose took the sopping clothes from off the step and set at the chore of scrubbing them. The barrel of water was still full near the line, and the task was a small price for the amusement Simon's tumble had provided.

Laundry water ran up her arms and over the front of her dress. She hummed amidst her smile. Though her life situation had taken a turn for the more mundane, Rose was quite sure she had never felt as content.

* * *

COLIN LABORED TO catch his breath and dismounted the horse. Riding had been the only method of curing his restlessness. For weeks, no word of Rose had come. He had inquired after her multiple times, sending letters to Grant Estate over and over, regardless of the curt replies he received by the hand of Prudence. Colin had written to Mrs. Ainsworth, Mrs. Lockhart, and even the local clergyman—all to no avail.

"No need to push the animal to exhaustion, Lord Stratfordshire," the groom said, taking the horse by the reins.

Colin staggered forward, petting his stallion around the neck. "I did not push him at all. In fact, the only thing I did was lose my hold and permit him to run freely."

"Of course, Lord Stratfordshire."

The stiff reply served as a summons. Colin straightened

and offered his gratitude before leaving the stable. He stopped just past the gate, surveying the estate.

He longed for another ride, perhaps twenty if they might ease his mind. He could not return to the house, not yet. His father, in an attempt to preoccupy him, had charged Colin with overseeing two new investments, and the task involved never-ending correspondence with the involved parties. The duke meant well, but Colin only grew more restless under the distraction.

Colin turned toward the gardens, determined to prolong his absence. He followed the paved path to the back garden. He passed the central fountain with its statues and the maze of hedges, continuing until he had walked more than half an hour into the flower gardens. He stopped at a patch of scented stocks, relishing in the sweet aroma. If only life were as simple as a garden—based upon simple rules of maintenance.

The garden walls reached four feet high, and the neighboring cottage peeked from the other side. Colin sat against an outer edge, listening to the hum of the woman set over the barrel of wash. Her voice carried across the breeze—blissfully gentle.

He sighed. He had come upon Rose in her kitchen garden on their second meeting and her voice had held a similar quality, only hers had held a haunting melancholy then.

The woman rung out a garment and turned to pin it to the line. The sight of her dark ringlets against her cheek, previously hidden from her bent over position, nearly choked him. He recognized those crimson lips and the dark lashes lining her hazel eyes.

Colin blinked furiously. He wiped at his eyes; they were playing a mean trick on him. He was overdone from his ride, and the heat of July threatened to suffocate his senses—or so he reasoned.

But there she stood, only yards away, humming her gentle song.

"Miss Grant," he said, before properly considering how he might approach her.

She jumped at his voice, dropping the garment to the grass. She bent to retrieve it. When she rose again, her cheeks blushed. "Lord Stratfordshire, I thought I might see you one of these days."

"One of these days?" He pushed himself over the wall, walking closer. "Have you been here all along?"

Rose's blush deepened, but she laughed amidst her embarrassment and offered a curtsy.

Colin stopped a few feet from her side, still distrusting his senses. For weeks he had tried to find Rose, and all the while she was just beyond the flower gardens at the cottage of his head gardener? Colin's brows drew together, and his heart raced at the reality. "Miss Grant, I tried to find you after the musicale, but you disappeared. I have spent some time searching for you."

She drew in a breath. "I am sorry. I had to leave my aunt, quite unexpectedly, to come and stay with my other aunt, Mrs. Amelia Rolland."

"Then you are related to my head gardener, Mr. Rolland?" Colin shook his head, trying to make sense of the scene before him.

Rose dipped her chin. "Yes. Mrs. Rolland is my mother's sister. Oliver is my cousin."

"Why did you not visit?"

Rose bit the bottom of her lip, and her cheeks seem to color for a third time. "I wished to, but I—I am afraid I ran away from home, you see, and I am staying within your servant's household. Seems an unlikely visitor for a future duke."

"Perhaps, but just as welcome, Miss Grant." His eyes

swept over her. The weeks since their last meeting had done her well—she looked happy. He paused at her hands; they were dirty and cracked near her knuckles. Colin took two steps closer. "Your hands."

Her hazel eyes rounded, and she hid her hands behind her back. "The effects of labor I suppose. I do not mind the work. My aunt and cousins are good to me, and so I enjoy helping in the household tasks. For the first time in my life, I feel rather useful."

"You look well."

"Do I?" She smiled, drying her hands against her apron. "What would you say if I told you that I quite wonder about my appearance?"

He smiled. "I would tell you not to wonder. You seem to play the part of country maid with surprising skill and charm."

"Thank you. But then, you have always been kind. I have not forgotten the service you provided me the night of the musicale. You were a true gentleman. I must return your handkerchief now that you have found me out."

Colin shook his head. Nervousness crept into his voice. "Now that I have found you out, I will not allow you to hide —not when I have a great many horses that need riding. Perhaps I might take you riding this week and show you around the farther gardens?"

"I would be glad to," Rose said, smiling.

Colin clasped his hands to keep from shaking. He was nearly certain his words sounded entirely too direct. "Does Friday suit you, Miss Grant? I can bring a horse and groom to the cottage."

She tilted her head, seeming to search his expression. "Yes, Friday would be lovely."

He took a wobbly step backward and bowed. His heartbeat pulsed in his ears. Friday could not come soon enough.

CHAPTER 8

The dirt road was narrow, surrounded by a thicket of trees on both sides. Overgrown brush encroached upon the path, and small purple flowers dotted the scene. Rose wiped at the small line of perspiration at the back of her neck and took in a deep breath.

"This is the plot," Colin said, patting the back of his horse. His navy coat contrasted drastically with his bright smile. His eyes had taken on the color of the wood—a gradient of different greens, shadows, and highlights. "My father has charged me with its improvement."

A pair of butterflies flitted across the path, and the soft breeze blew against the treetops, rustling the leaves. "I cannot imagine how you would."

His lips tugged, and he pulled his reins. "I quite agree. Stratfordshire has more than enough fountains, ponds, and manicured gardens. Sometimes I think this place is the only piece of property that remains untouched by time."

"Then you do not wish to clear the land?" Rose could not imagine trading such a space for an organized and manmade imitation. The land's beauty lay in its wildness, its unruly and spontaneous nature—a broken log here, a patch of flowers there, the interlacing tree canopies, and the fragments of light shining to the forest floor. The area smelled of childhood—tree sap and flowers, mixed with the muskiness of the thicket.

Colin shook his head. "Would you walk with me instead? The horses could use a rest, and the groom will not be far."

She clasped her hands to her chest and laughed. "I was hoping you might ask. Riding is among my favorites, Lord Stratfordshire, but exploring on such a day as today seems even lovelier."

They dismounted, and the groom came to collect their horses.

"There is something I thought to show you," Colin began, offering his arm.

Rose stepped on the uneven ground, balancing against the marquess's arm when needed. The terrain was filled with pockets and bumps, each one an obstacle in her stiff riding boots. Spraining an ankle would be a sure way to embarrass herself.

He led her around a wall of shrubs, where a pile of wood had been placed in a lean-to arrangement. The log and sticks were dried and splintered, and ivy ran between the cracks and around the supporting tree trunk.

A smile touched her lips. "Is this from—did you make this?"

"Yes, years ago." Colin drew his arm away and crouched near the small opening. He removed his hat and chuckled. His shoulders shook from the effort, and his brown waves glimmered with the spotted light from above. "Believe it or not, I use to play in this fort often. I imagined I was a part of the militia or sailing on exploratory assignments from the queen herself."

Rose bit the edge of her bottom lip to keep from laughing.

She could well imagine him as a boy, pretending. She supposed he seemed much the same as he did right then, carefree with disheveled dark waves.

Colin stood, turning back to her. "I suppose that is why my father charged me with the keep of the land. He knew of my sentiment, and yet, I cannot seem to imagine anything else in this place. No number of hedges or stones can improve it."

"I understand quite well," Rose said, leaning a hand against the trunk of a nearby tree. "But, as I have learned, places do not hold memories—people do."

His eyes flickered to hers with such admiration that her breath nearly caught in her chest. "Exactly so."

Rose's pulse quickened. She tried to steady herself, tracing her finger around the knots in the tree. "However, you needn't clear the land to please your father. Just as land cannot hold memories, neither should it be altered for the sake of being altered. Perhaps you could clear the dead trees and add paths for the horses, all the while maintaining the essence of this place."

"An excellent idea again." Colin's voice commanded her gaze.

Their eyes met, and when a smile lit his cheeks, Rose's knees threatened to give out.

He bent and plucked a purple flower, handing it to her. His voice grew gentle. "These are my favorite flowers in all of Stratfordshire, even more than the scented stocks. These flowers grow wild, and some of the gardeners consider them a weed, but I do not."

She tucked the floret in her pocket. "I adore collecting flowers. They make any room brighter. My Aunt Prudence detests them. She says they are altogether too fragrant and dry up too quickly."

Colin searched her face. "You are nothing like your aunt,

in looks nor temperament."

Rose's brows furrowed. "The other day, when I told you that I wondered at my appearance..."

"Yes?"

She inhaled sharply. "Prudence forbade mirrors in my home. The only glimpses of my reflection came from a silver pitcher or the occasional puddle of water."

"You..." Colin's eyes rounded, and his fingers tapped against his sides. "But surely you looked into a mirror before your mother passed?"

"Perhaps, but I was young and more interested in the gardens and sitting on the lap of my mother. My grandfather, as you are already aware, is blind, but he had his own way of looking at me. He used to touch my face, and he told me how I resembled my father." Rose let out a shaky breath. Her lungs almost felt as restricted as they had the night of the musicale. Speaking of Prudence and her mother and grand-father brought a stab of pain in her abdomen. "I used to walk the hall of family portraits, studying the lot of them, wondering how I might compare."

"But surely you have seen your reflection in a shop window...?"

She bit her lip. Prudence had only allowed her chaper-oned trips to town; she seemed bent on preventing Rose from seeing her reflection.

His jaw dropped, but he quickly recovered. Colin shuf-fled forward. "Then you are unaware of how—you do not know?"

She pressed her lips together and shook her head.

Colin's cheeks warmed, and his lips tugged at the corners. "Miss Grant, you are every bit as charming as any flower in this field. Your eye color seems to change with your mood—one moment green with flecks of gold and another gray at the edges and brown in the center. I am sure you have ascertained your complexion light, your hair dark as night. And your lips—crimson."

Rose felt frozen in place, mesmerized by his words but even more by the way he looked at her. She was certain no man had regarded her with so much warmth. She swallowed. "Thank you for the description, Lord Stratfordshire. I will have to find a mirror, now that I am no longer under Prudence's roof."

"Yes, you must," Colin said, tucking one of her curls behind her ear. His hand lingered near her cheek, and his gaze continued to sweep over her.

Her cheeks burned impossibly hot. Was it normal to feel so lightheaded in the presence of a friend? Her rushed breathing and tight chest seemed to answer for her.

"Your Grace," the groom said, calling from across the wall of hedges. "You asked me to warn you when the time passed noon."

Colin lifted a hand in the air. "Thank you, Stephen."

Rose's chest caved. The sensations flooding her senses frightened her, yet returning to the horses and retreating from his nearness sparked immediate disappointment too.

"Miss Grant?" Colin asked.

She swallowed and accepted his outstretched arm. Surely he could hear her heart knocking against her chest or the way her breath refused to steady itself. They reached the path and mounted their horses, and Rose wondered if Colin felt as she did.

"I wondered if you might be up for a race?" Colin asked when the silence grew too thick.

"A race?" Rose could not contain her surprise. Perhaps the marquess meant to diffuse the tension. "I am always game for sport, Lord Stratfordshire."

His eyes flashed with pride. "I hoped you would agree."

Rose kicked to a gallop and full on sprint, leaning toward

the front of the saddle. She flew across the path, and a quick backward glance brought on a spell of laughter. Rose's horse kicked up clumps of mud directly at the marquess. He, however, looked not the least deterred, pulling in line with her horse. They rode the entire route back to the cottage in similar suit. One moment Rose would pull ahead, but then Colin would take the lead.

Her cheeks ached from smiling by the time he walked her to the front steps. His cheeks were splattered in dots of mud, and he looked much like the boy she had imagined in the thicket.

"May I call on you again?" Colin asked, bowing over her. His voice was warm and deep.

Rose offered her hand, still smiling. "I would like that very much, Lord Stratfordshire."

He grasped her fingers in his own, sending a wave of warmth up her arm. "Until then, and in the meantime, you are free to roam the gardens."

NOT EVEN A DAY passed before Colin saw Rose again. On his morning ride, he paused near the orchard to adjust his stirrup, and between the thick rows of trees, each one covered in ripening fruit, stood the enchanting woman.

Rose strolled the aisles, brushing her fingers through the tangle of branches and leaves and stopping every so often to inspect an apple. Unaware of his presence, she continued her walk. Colin smiled when he recognized her soft humming; that was at least the third time he had caught her singing.

He climbed down from his horse and called to her. "Miss Grant."

She jumped, knocking a few apples from the tree and onto the ground. "Lord Stratfordshire," she said, bending to retrieve the apples. "Do you make it a habit of startling young ladies?"

"Only lately." His laughter caused a blush to spread against her cheeks. He wrapped his reins around the trunk of the nearest tree. "I take it you have made a habit of walking the orchard. You seemed lost in thought. Are you well?"

Her head bobbed up and down. "I was only thinking of my home. I left under difficult circumstances. I worry about my grandfather and my aunt…"

A set of birds swooped between them and into the tangle of branches. Colin took the moment to bury the disappointment that threatened. He'd only just found her, and he did not want to lose her again. "Then you are considering returning home?"

She lifted one of the apples in her hands and smelled it before answering. "I have, but I cannot leave Aunt Amelia and my cousins so soon after years of absence."

Colin's lips tugged; she would not be leaving yet.

Rose handed him an apple. "Tell me, Lord Stratfordshire, how do you know when the apple is ripe?"

He bit into the fruit in response. His lips puckered; the tartness curled his tongue. He swallowed it whole, but the chunk lodged in his throat, nearly choking him. "Not ready," he said in a raspy voice.

Rose's lips threatened laughter, but her eyes surveyed him carefully. "Are you well?"

He laughed amidst his embarrassment, causing a bout of coughing. He admired her restraint; he was certain he appeared every bit as ridiculous as he felt. "Yes. Unfortunately, you cannot judge the fruit by appearance alone. That bite was enough to poison even the most devoted apple lover."

Her resolve seemed to crack, and she laughed. The sound was freedom itself—joyful, uninhibited, and magical. Colin had to catch his breath. He could not recall feeling so at ease and happy with another person.

She studied the apple that remained in her hands. "True. This apple does look ready, and it even smells ready. I wonder..." She drew in a breath and took a bite. Her eyes, nearly brown this morning, widened, and the lines near her brows softened. "Practically perfect, Lord Stratfordshire."

"That is the fickleness of apples, Miss Grant. Two may grow beside each other, receiving the same sunlight and water and attention from the gardener. They make look similar, even smell similar, but inside? That is the mystery of both man and fruit."

Her laughter subsided. Her steps slowed. "I like to think every apple, or person, will sweeten in due time. Perhaps some just take longer?"

There was hope in her words, maybe even pleading. New lines appeared at the side of each eye, and her lips fell downward.

An ache pulsed in his throat, and he considered his response. Colin understood wishing to see the best in others, but he had the distinct impression that Rose spoke of Prudence. From his two encounters with Rose's aunt and the stories he had heard, Prudence Grant would need miraculous ripening if she were ever to come close to sweet.

He offered a weak smile, trying to ignore the piles of rotten apples at the foot of the tree. "Only time may tell."

Rose pushed back her bonnet, allowing the sun to light her face fully. The effect caused Colin's heart to thump at an unhealthy speed. She still did not know her beauty; she still did not understand how lovely a person she was—physically or otherwise.

She cleared her throat and her cheeks colored. She seemed aware of his silent admiration, or, at the very least, uncomfortable with the silence that had spread between them. She lifted her chin. "I am off to see Oliver. On unseasonably warm days like today, he appreciates the visits. I always bring some of my aunt's jam tartlets. Would you care for one?"

Heat radiated through his chest, and he glanced back at his horse, happily munching on the fallen fruit. "Thank you, but I have had enough tartness for today."

Rose laughed once more, though the sound was softer and more guarded.

"Do thank your cousin for me. The orchard has never looked better." Colin stared at her, hoping she felt his meaning. His attempt felt clumsy. "And I hope you will still allow me to call on you in a few days?"

A cloud lifted, and a ray of sunshine hit her head on. Golden flecks lit her eyes. "I will look forward to it."

Colin bowed and returned to his horse with a smile. He had always felt drawn to the orchard with its sweet smell and solitude, but now, he marked it as his favorite place on the estate—even above his childhood wood.

CHAPTER 9

"You cannot tell me his interest is only out of friendship. No young man asks to call at the cottage of his gardener. Such things are just not done, Rose." Amelia threaded her embroidery needle and knotted the end. "Don't you agree, Oliver?"

The cottage parlor became the gathering place each evening. The green velvet sofa, the bookshelf scant with books, the cozy fire, and the warm voices—Rose had never felt safer.

Simon and Eli read their books and practiced their arithmetic at the kitchen table religiously, just outside the front room's opening, and Oliver sprawled against the back of the sofa and begged Rose to play the pianoforte. The instrument had seen better days—the notes did not hold and often fell flat—but Rose was happy to indulge him most evenings.

But tonight, Aunt Amelia had decided to provide conversation—conversation that concerned Rose and the marquess. The attention discomfited Rose, but she also could not help adoring it. Never had she shared such intimate conversations with family; never had she felt so cared for.

"The situation is complicated, Mother." Oliver stroked his chin. His stubble had multiplied in the past week, and he was on his way to acquiring a handsome beard. "Rose is the daughter of a gentleman, the granddaughter of a baron, but she is residing here. I have heard much talk of honor and duty while at Stratfordshire. I cannot believe the duke would risk gossip for the opportunity to court Rose—no matter how handsome she is."

Rose's chest hitched. Oliver was right. The marquess might have considered her, had she not fled from Prudence. He might have courted her. But now? The situation had grown problematic. She stared at her dry and cracked hands, trying to scrape the bits of dirt from beneath her nails. Her situation, though infinitely preferable to that of Prudence's guardianship, had taken a turn for the worse when it came to the marriage market.

"Nonsense." Amelia dropped her embroidery to the side. "Rose is just as proper a choice as before. You may be a gardener, Oliver, but I am a widow of a soldier. That means something to anyone that cares about this country."

Eli's chair scooted across the floorboards. "I can hardly study with your chattering. Might as well share in the discussion."

Rose laughed, but she shook her head. "I won't hear any more of this. I did not come here to become the topic of the evening. Now, continue with your studies, Eli and Simon."

Oliver readjusted his position, jabbing Rose with his elbow. "A song might be enough to quiet my mother and me, at least for now."

A rap at the door startled them both. Oliver rose, crinkling his brows. "Saved only by a mysterious visitor." He swung open the door. Oliver's shoulders suddenly went rigid, and he bowed. "Lord Stratfordshire, to what do I owe this pleasure?"

Amelia's eyes bulged and she stood, swiping a hand over her hair.

The marquess's baritone voice carried across the room. "I apologize for disturbing you, Mr. Rolland."

"Lord Stratfordshire, do come in," Amelia said, walking to the door. She shot Rose a look of urgency. "Rose was just putting on the kettle for tea."

Rose stood, offering a stiff curtsy at Colin in the doorway. She felt the weight of her cousins' stares. The entire room seemed to close in, and she felt insufferably hot. She could not help feeling their gossip had summoned Colin.

Colin fiddled with the hat in his hands. He stared at Rose, though his words were directed to Amelia. "I would not mean to inconvenience you, Mrs. Rolland, but tea does sound wonderful after the ride."

Rose dipped her chin. "I'll get the tea started."

She disappeared around the corner and nearly collapsed against the hearth. Her heart threatened to tear through her chest. She could not decide which factor led to her condition —the surprise of seeing Colin at the cottage or her cousins' wide eyes and grins. Her hands shook as she poured the water into the kettle, spilling the liquid over top and onto the front of her dress. She dropped the pitcher of water, and shrieked.

"Rose, is everything all right in there?" Amelia said from the parlor.

Rose swatted at the water on her skirt. She bit her bottom lip to keep from smiling. There was only one reason she should be so jumpy at his arrival. She fanned her cheeks, allowing herself to breath freely. "I am coming, Aunt—just now."

She returned to the parlor, only ten steps from the kitchen archway. The marquess still stood near the front door, and he looked unsure of the protocol. "Miss Grant, I was just explaining to your aunt. I found your cousin's hat in the orchard just now and thought to return it to him."

"Tonight?" Simon asked from the kitchen. His dark hair covered his eyes, but Rose recognized the teasing glint in them. "Ollie often loses track of his hats. He has at least five he rotates."

Eli snickered. "But how would the marquess know, Simon? He's simply being a good neighbor."

Colin extended the hat to Oliver rigidly. "Mr. Rolland, I apologize for interrupting your evening." He turned to Rose and bowed. "Forgive me, Miss Grant, Mrs. Rolland. Continue with your evening."

"Wait." Rose clasped her hands. Now that she had seen him, she did not want him to leave.

"Yes?" he asked, straightening.

She smiled. "The tea won't be long. Please, sit with us."

The marquess arched a brow, looking to the twins at the table. He rocked on his back leg. "I would not wish to impose—"

"Goodness, no." Oliver offered a hand. "I was just pleading with my cousin to favor us with some music. Have you had a chance to hear her sing or play yet, Lord Stratfordshire?"

"Miss Grant?" Colin's shoulders pulled back, and his confidence seemed to return. "I have not, Mr. Rolland, but not for lack of trying. I attended a musicale with your cousin over a month ago. She was to perform but left early due to a headache. I have wondered about her talent ever since."

Aunt Amelia scowled at Rose. "You never told me you had met the marquess before—"

"The musicale at Milton Manor, Aunt—the one I spoke to you about at my arrival." Rose bit her lip. She had told Amelia about Prudence and the corset, but not about Colin.

She feared doing so would betray her interest in the marquess. Rose gestured to the chair. "Lord Stratfordshire."

Amusement flickered across his eyes, but he obediently sat.

"Rose, you may play for Lord Stratfordshire, and I will finish the tea." Amelia smiled widely at Colin. "My niece does play beautifully."

Rose strode past Colin and sat the pianoforte. Playing music was infinitely preferable to that of the twins' teasing glances or the flutters she felt whenever Colin glanced her direction. She stretched her fingers and straightened her back and allowed her hands to sink into the starting chord of Ignaz Pleyel's *Sinfonia Concertante Ben. 112.*

When she ended, the small room erupted with cheers.

"Marvelous," Oliver said, offering to assist her from the bench.

Rose grinned, in part relief the song had finished and in part to her cousin's compliment. She accepted his outstretched hand. "Thank you, Oliver. Now that you have had your song, perhaps you will allow me to drink my tea in peace."

Her cousin nodded. "That is only fair."

"Miss Grant, you play beautifully—" Colin's statement hung, and Rose was sure there was something more he wished to say.

"But?" she said, smiling.

Colin laughed. "But I had hoped to hear you sing."

"That," Rose said, sitting at her usual place on the sofa, "will have to come another day."

"Then I shall have to fetch your cousin's hat again." Colin crossed his legs, and his lips seemed to hint at a smile.

Amelia entered the room with the tray, the cups and saucers tinkling together. Her cheeks held an uncharacteristic rosiness. She settled the tea against the small table and poured the first cup. "Now, what have I missed?"

Oliver chuckled and ran his fingers through his auburn waves. "The marquess and Rose were just discussing how we must do this again."

Rose's cheeks pinched. She dipped her chin. "Yes, I rather think we should."

WHAT HAD STARTED as an occasional visit turned into daily routine. More than once, Colin had set out for a solitary walk, only to find himself standing at the steps of the Rolland cottage. At times he searched for an excuse, *any* excuse—a misplaced gardening cap, a pair of sheers kept from the shed —to join the Rolland's evening meetings in the cottage parlor.

On his third visit to the cottage, Colin heard Rose sing. Just as he expected, her voice lacked the customary embellishments and pretense. Rather, Rose's voice carried across the notes as easily and effortlessly as everything else she did.

Their walks, their rides, their every conversation continued to convince Colin; he was quite in love with Rose.

Colin studied her now, watching as the sun lit her cheeks. Their current turn around the flower garden had been as enjoyable as their other meetings.

He knew what others would say—he had attached himself to a lady staying in one of his servant's household! But Rose was a proper lady in every sense of the word. She was mannered and well spoken; she was kind, almost to a fault. And like a flower, she had grown unaware of the beauty she emitted. The longer she stayed with the Rolland household, the more at ease she seemed to become. Her laughter came easier with each of their meetings.

"Sunflowers," Colin said, breaking into a smile. "That is the plant I would compare you to."

Rose sat on a bench and laughed. "I imagine your answer has something to do with this bonnet."

Her bonnet was indeed yellow, a pale but cheerful color that complimented her dark hair and eyes perfectly. But Colin shook his head. "I suppose I might have answered too hastily. Haven't you noticed how the flowers turn toward the sun? I believe you see more good than bad in every person you meet. Do you even notice the darkness?"

She winced. "I do notice the darkness, more than I let on, I'm afraid. Often, I ignore it for far too long…as was the case with Prudence."

"It is difficult to see darkness in those that we wish to see light." Colin sat beside her, nodding at the groom a few feet away.

"A tree."

"Pardon?" A broad grin stretched across his face. "You are comparing me to a tree?"

Rose's nose crinkled, and laughter slipped from her perfect lips. "You are rather tall, Lord Stratfordshire. Besides, a tree is as good as any plant. Have you ever stepped into the shade of a tree on a particularly hot day?"

Colin grasped at his side. He could not resist teasing her when she laughed. "Then I am good for shade?"

One of her brow's lifted. "You are rooted and upright and surprisingly comfortable to be around."

"Comfortable?" He inched closer.

Her cheeks colored, as they did each time he drew nearer.

He pulled out a parcel from his coat pocket. He had been carrying it for their walk, waiting for the right moment to give it to her. After only a brief meeting and a couple weeks of visits, Colin was sure of his affection. The rapidity of his feelings startled him. He never would have supposed he might know a prospective partner's character on such short notice. Was it possible that Rose felt the same for him in such a short duration?

"What is that?" Rose asked.

Colin laid it in her upturned hands. "For you. I thought you should have this after our talk a couple weeks ago."

She gave a tentative smile, seeming to contemplate. "Lord Stratfordshire—"

"Please." His pulse pounded in his ears in anticipation.

Rose drew back the paper and pulled out the handheld mirror. Her eyes filled with emotion. "A mirror."

He touched her hand, clearing his throat. "I thought you should see your reflection properly, any day you wish to."

She traced her fingers around the golden handle, and a tear slipped down her cheek. "Thank you."

"Well? Aren't you going to look in it?"

She laughed amidst her misty eyes, wiping a hand against her moistened cheeks. "I have longed to see my reflection for years, but now that I am holding a mirror—this remarkably beautiful one, I should add—I hesitate. What if I do not like what I see?"

"You will never know until you look," Colin said, taking the mirror from her hands. He lifted it higher, until it sat level with her gaze.

She gasped, and her fingers flew to her face, tracing the features of her reflection.

His mouth went dry, and his voice cracked. "As I said, your eyes change with your mood. They are greener with your tears. I failed to mention your lashes, though you can see how thick and long they are now. And your lips…"

She pressed her hand to his shoulder, shaking with a watery sob. Her eyes clamped shut.

Colin lowered the mirror. Had he done something wrong? Did she fail to see the beauty that was so obvious to him? "Miss Grant, if I have done something to cause offense—"

"No." She met his eyes. Her lips curved upward despite her tears. "It is only—I had not expected... I look like her. I look like my mother. I cannot tell you how many times I have stared at her portrait, wishing I carried a piece of her with me. But in my wildest imaginings, I had not thought I resembled her so closely."

Relief washed over his anxiety, and he exhaled, touching her damp cheek. "Your mother must have been very lovely indeed."

Rose visibly swallowed. Her lips trembled. "Thank you. You cannot know how much this means to me."

Colin shrugged. "I gave you nothing but a mirror."

"You restored a part of her—my mother," Rose said, rising to her feet. Her eyes still shone with emotion, but her tears slowed. "You have my gratitude forever."

CHAPTER 10

To Miss Rose Grant and Mrs. Amelia Rolland,

You are cordially invited to a ball on Friday, the 12th of August at Stratfordshire. Festivities begin at 8 o' clock in the evening. Please send word of your attendance at your earliest convenience.

Warmest Regards,

The Duke and Duchess of Andover

"Reading over the invitation again?" Amelia asked, kneading the bread against the tabletop. She laughed and shook her head. "Can you imagine a duke inviting the mother of his gardener to a ball? I thought I had lived to see all ridiculousness."

Rose set the invitation back to the mantle. As a child, she had dreamed of dancing and balls and gentlemen, but those hopes had vanished with the arrival of Prudence. Her aunt had closeted Rose until she had no longer received invitations. But now? She smiled, trying to recall the dance steps her governess had taught her years ago in the Grant Estate ballroom.

"Does the duke imagine me capable of buying a ballgown?" Amelia said, laughing. She tucked a stray hair behind her ear, leaving a trail of flour in its place.

Despite Amelia's best efforts, Rose saw through the protests; her aunt was thrilled, elated even, to be included on the invitation list of the Duke of Andover. Rose's cheeks pinched. "Perhaps you are right. Shall I dictate our regrets?"

"Now, wait," Amelia said, sticking her tongue into the side of her cheek. Her forehead scrunched together, and she tapped a finger to her chin. "I would so hate to disappoint the duke, particularly after his kindness in hiring Oliver. The marquess would be heartbroken if you were not there... Allowances are made with matters of the heart, you know."

Rose placed her hands on her hips. "Now, Aunt!"

Amelia's lips twitched. "I may not be able to afford a dress, but there may be something we can do."

"I have more than enough to buy you fabric," Rose offered. "And you are the daughter of a dressmaker. Surely you remember something of sewing and patterns and the like? I would offer you one of my gowns if I thought one might fit."

"Surely." Amelia hands sunk into the dough once more, but this time she stayed there, frozen in thought. "Did I fail to mention I have some old dresses? With some embellishment and alterations, one of those might do nicely."

A surge of warmth encompassed Rose. She had been nervous to leave her childhood home, nervous to lose the little memory she had of her mother. Without her mother's portrait, how would Rose remember?

However, coming to Andover continued to restore pieces —more than Rose could have anticipated. First with Amelia's kindness and laughter, then her cousin's adventurous spirit, and, most touching, the marquess's gifted mirror. Each portion combined into a greater picture than the one hanging at the Grant Estate, for this new portrait of her mother was not one of oil and canvas but of a living, breathing memory, a feeling and spirit more tangible than sight.

"Then you will come?" Rose asked, teetering forward.

Amelia laughed. "Certainly, my dear."

Rose flew across the room to embrace her aunt. She pulled Amelia closer, resting her cheek against hers. "Do you suppose happiness such as mine can last? I can scarcely breathe for fear of it fading away."

Her aunt pulled back, placing a floured hand at Rose's cheek. Her dark eyes seemed to sparkle. "For the daughter of Lillian—yes. For one with your fair heart, most assuredly."

The cottage door swung open, and Rose retreated from her aunt's arms.

Oliver stood at the front of the room. His brawny shoulders pulled back, and he took off his hat. His freckled cheeks lifted. "Mother, I have news to share."

Amelia resumed kneading the dough. "I would expect so, considering you are here at this hour. Aren't you needed in the gardens?"

"Not today." Oliver combed through his disheveled auburn locks. His dark eyes seemed to dance. "The marquess paid me a visit today. He inquired about your attendance at the ball in a week."

"And?" Amelia interrupted. "What did you say?"

Oliver sighed, shaking a finger. "Mother, would you allow me to finish the story?"

She shrugged. "Carry on."

"I said I knew nothing of such things, and he called me to his study in the house. There, he granted me a nearly two weeks bonus and the day off. He insisted I take the pair of you shopping in town today for the ball."

Rose clutched her hands to her chest. "Lord Stratfordshire is too kind. I hope you did not accept such a payment. Oliver?"

Her cousin tossed his hat to the hook. "The marquess left me no choice. Of course I rejected the offer at first. I have country pride," Oliver said, casting a teasing gleam in Rose's direction. "But then, Lord Stratfordshire pled. He remarked that your attendance is especially hoped for, Rose. I countered that we would find a way to have you there without his charity, but…"

The room fell silent.

"But?" Amelia asked.

Rose blinked rapidly. Colin had been kind to her, kinder than she deserved. He had searched for her for weeks when she had fled to Andover; he continued to call and beg her company.

Hopes rolled together like a giant snowball—building and building—until Rose's expectations of her future with Colin were impossibly large. She knew better than to expect an offer. He was the future Duke of Andover; Rose, despite being the granddaughter of a baron, was staying in the cottage of a head gardener. But this news of the ball—Colin's interest in her attendance—sparked the prospect once again.

Oliver stared at Rose, and his eyes seemed to shine with pride. "But I could not refuse him, Mother. The way he spoke about Rose left little doubt in my mind."

Oh dear. Rose's heart banged against her chest, and her throat started to close in. Oliver was wiser than his years—he had to be to secure his position at Stratfordshire—and if he thought that Colin would make an offer…

Rose shook her head. She could not afford to believe such a thing. Happiness like hers could not endure, did not; Prudence had squashed that dream long ago.

"I think I shall take a walk," Rose said, pushing past Oliver to retrieve her bonnet from the side of the door.

Oliver touched her arm. "But we are to go to town to go shopping, Rose. I have strict orders."

She closed her eyes. "Yes, of course, but only after I take a moment to collect my thoughts."

* * *

THE DUCHESS DID NOT LIFT the fork from the table. Her cheeks looked uncommonly pale, and the line of perspiration near her hairline worried Colin. His mother had been far too extended—caring for the Smith family and preparing for the ball in the coming week.

"Mother, you are unwell." Colin set his napkin to the side of his plate and stood. With his mother's condition of the lungs, every sickness—even a slight cold—made room for worry.

The duchess shook her head. "Nothing to trouble yourself with, son. I was in contact with Mrs. Smith's boy far too often, but it was only a cold, pneumonia at worst."

"At worst?" Colin frowned. "Mother, pneumonia could be your undoing. You must return to bed. I will call the doctor straight away. Where is father?"

She clutched the edge of the table, avoiding his gaze. "He went out on business yesterday. I expect him back today. Colin, I have much to do in preparation. Summer End's ball is the highlight of my year at Stratfordshire."

He returned to his seat. His mother refused to rest whenever illness came, and usually her will power was enough to carry her through. Still, her coughing only worsened, and the state of her lungs were in constant jeopardy.

"Has Miss Grant responded to her invitation to the ball?" The duchess asked, taking a sip of her tea.

Colin scratched the fork at his plate. "I believe she will, though I have not heard directly."

The duchess coughed into her napkin. She offered a smile once she recovered. "Then you will ask her for her hand?"

"I had hoped to do so, informally at least... You do not object, do you?"

Colin had been nervous to tell his mother. He was sure of his attachment, sure of Rose's character, but his mother acted strange each time he left to call on Rose—fidgeting endlessly, avoiding his gaze, and never inquiring about his visits upon his return.

"I have no objections, as long as you are sure, Colin."

He swallowed hard, setting his fork against the plate. The delicate swirls on the porcelain china seemed the perfect illustration for his thoughts. "And your hesitance to answer does not have to do with whatever happened at the musicale, does it? You still have refused to tell me."

The duchess winced. "What happened at the musicale— you are still fixated on it? Miss Grant had a headache, nothing more. I spoke with her briefly in an adjoining room and urged her to return home if it did not improve."

Colin's jaw jutted forward. Her attempts at deception had not improved; she was hiding something. He wanted to pound his fist on the table and ask, but he refrained. His mother had too many demands weighing on her health. He would not add to her suffering by persisting in asking for an answer.

"But I have not been able to place my comb from that night." The duchess scowled. "First Miss Grant's headache and then the loss of my most precious possession—Mrs. Ainsworth presents quite the program."

Colin sighed. "And Mrs. Ainsworth still has not found it?"

His mother had received the comb as a wedding present from Colin's father. The golden comb was adorned with rubies and engravings in the shape of apple trees—meant to symbolize the orchard at Stratfordshire, where the duke had asked for her hand in marriage some twenty-seven years previous.

"No, but things are not always as they seem. I believe it still might turn up." The duchess offered a weak smile.

Colin returned her smile, if only to appease her. The comb was worth more than most received annually. If someone had taken it, the comb was not likely to be returned any time soon.

ose held back the mirror, admiring the blue silk of her new gown. She still had not grown accustomed to her reflection or the image of her mother shining back at her. Her brows furrowed, and she studied the effect.

Mirrors had not always been forbidden. There was a time, before Prudence's arrival at Grant Estate, when reflections were nothing to be talked—or ashamed—about. Maybe that was why Rose had never thought to study her own. What she had remembered from her childhood likeness was sparse and discouraging—mousy brown hair, eyes and legs she had not grown into yet, and freckles. Time had transformed Rose. She had already known her hair had turned darker, but the spots along her upper cheeks had faded, and her face had morphed into that of her mother's.

She caught a glimpse of Simon in the mirror. He laughed. "You look just the part of a future duchess, cousin."

Rose's cheeks burned red. She still had not allowed herself to hope. The possible disappointment seemed insurmountable. She had never wished for something more than she wished for a future with Colin. "Simon—"

"Enough," Amelia said, pushing the final pins in Rose's elaborate twists and curls. "Do not tease her so. She will not catch anyone's eye if she is to turn into a blushing and blubbering girl. Now, tell your cousin how well she looks."

Simon conceded, and his head lowered. "Rose, you look very well."

"Thank you. Now was that so difficult?" Amelia asked, shooing him from the room. She rested her hands atop Rose's shoulders. "A fifteen-year-old boy knows nothing of compliments. You look more than well, Rose. You are enchanting. And there is only one more thing to be done."

Rose looked up at her aunt in question.

"Oliver?" Amelia called across the house. When her oldest son appeared in the doorway, she nodded. "Would you be so kind to bring me the package I found on the doorstep two days ago?"

He folded his arms, and his rounded shoulders flexed. "Are you sure that is wise? It came without tag or any note. After what happened with the corset, I wonder if it is another trick…"

Rose's aunt sighed. "There is only one person, besides the king himself, that I know can afford such a trinket, and considering how handsomely *he* paid you to take us shopping, I have little doubt for whom the gift was intended. Oliver, the box."

"As you wish, Mother." He stalked from the room, returning with a wooden box. He shifted his weight, seeming to deliberate.

Amelia's eyes narrowed.

"Right, here you are, Rose," Oliver said, handing it over.

The wood was smooth to the touch. Rose flipped open the hinged top and gasped. Inside lay the most enchanting piece of art she had ever seen—a golden comb with engravings of tree branches and red jewels as the apples. Her heart sped. *The orchard.* Colin knew how she loved that place. They had spoken about it on their last walk.

"Rose, do you think it is from Lord Stratfordshire?" Oliver asked.

"Yes." She nodded her head and smiled. "He knows how I loved the orchard, and he has spoken about how the place— your employment—has brought us together once again."

Oliver craned his neck. "Then he has intentions to ask for your hand."

She clutched the comb to her chest. Colin's affection suddenly seemed obvious—the way his eyes lit up each time he saw her, their daily visits in the gardens or on horse-back, the mirror, the new ball gown, his kind compliments. Even more convincing were her own sensations. Colin's slightest touch could induce a record pounding of her heart, a wave of warmth, and a happiness she had not known existed. She loved him, and she could no longer believe the attachment was one sided. Logic would not allow.

"He might." Rose turned to her aunt. Emotion glistened in her eyes.

Amelia wrapped an arm around Rose's shoulder and kissed her forehead. "I urge you to trust in your heart. Lord Stratfordshire cares for you. His attention cannot be mistaken. You will be the future duchess of Andover, if you so desire."

Oliver's lips pursed, and a line near his brows appeared. Rose recognized his contemplation. "You should expect a proposal, Rose. Lord Stratfordshire would never have sent such a gift otherwise."

"Then…" Rose's lips parted, and a shaky sigh escaped. She caved into her aunt's arms. Doubt slipped away with each contented tear. After years of isolation, Providence had granted her a new future. "Nothing would make me happier than marrying Lord Stratfordshire. He is the most honorable man I have ever met."

Amelia pulled away. "Then dry those tears. We must leave for the ball, but only after I put the comb in your hair."

Rose nodded her approval, and Amelia worked the gift into the side of her hair.

The duke himself sent his finest carriage to collect the two women. The red velvet seating and golden trimmed interior sent Amelia into ramblings. *"When you are duchess..."* *"Can you imagine your wedding?"* *"You do look lovely when you smile."* *"I have always thought the marquess the most handsome man in Andover."*

Rose cheeks ached by the time they approached the drive to Stratfordshire. With each breath, her confidence grew, and when the footmen delivered her down the carriage and onto the front drive, Rose's complexion glowed, and her eyes lit with excitement.

She nearly toppled over. For all her and Colin's meetings, Rose had not seen the house so closely. Colin had not prepared her for the sight.

Stratfordshire was the jewel of the entire county, and likely much of England. The house, which had been the palace for many past kings, was built of white stone and composed of multiple towers. The copper roofs varied in shape—domes and points and elongated trapezoidal prisms —each with castle spires reaching into the sky. The sunset only added to the grandness. Pinks and oranges burned behind the house, and the final rays of sunlight cast a glow around it.

Not even St. James' Palace in Westminster or Queens House in London could compare in Rose's estimation. She fiddled with her pendant necklace.

Amelia's hand slipped through Rose's arm. Her aunt

visibly swallowed. "I have only seen the house from afar. I think I shall faint."

Her aunt's dramatics brought a hint of relief. Rose smiled. "You will be at ease when you meet the duke and duchess and marquess. They are warm and welcoming, I assure you."

They entered the large hall and were ushered into the grand ballroom.

"Rose, have you ever seen such grandness?" Amelia asked when they stepped into the domed room.

Columns lined the round area, and gold-leaf covered each embellishment along the ceiling and walls. Chandeliers with candles cast charming shadows across the ceiling, lighting below. And the flowers. The groups of pastel bouquets near each window and door served to scent the entire room.

Words escaped Rose. She stood, mouth agape, watching as the couples swirled around the dance floor. Colin had always treated her as an equal, a friend, but seeing his home and the luxury it offered... Rose pulled at her gloves, thankful they covered her cracked and dried skin. Running back to the cottage seemed entirely tempting.

No wonder Prudence had been perpetually dissatisfied with their home; little surprise she had schemed so desperately for a place alongside the duke. For someone set on the vain things of the world, Stratfordshire was the ultimate prize. In fact, even a sincere woman would find rejecting such an offer difficult.

Rose's mother must have loved her father dearly.

The duke met Rose's gaze from a few yards away, and he smiled, waving her closer.

She met him with a curtsy. "Your Grace."

He took her hand in his, kissing it lightly. He wore a blue sash around his coat, and medals adorned his chest. "Miss Grant, I have been looking forward to seeing you again. I still hear talk of your rescuing me that day in the shepherd's field.

I am not sure which creature was more helpless—me or that lamb you carried."

She laughed. "Certainly the lamb, Your Grace. Have you met my aunt? Please allow me the honor of introducing Mrs. Amelia Rolland."

Amelia blushed and offered a clumsy attempt at a curtsy. For all her easy conversation, she seemed quite awestruck. She dipped her head. "Your Grace."

The duke, seemingly aware of her nerves, swooped Amelia's hand and placed a kiss on it as he had for Rose. "Mrs. Rolland, I consider it a pleasure to meet any friend of your niece. Welcome to Stratfordshire. I do hope you enjoy your evening."

Rose searched the line for the duchess. As hostess, she would not miss greeting her guests.

"My wife is currently taking a rest near the refreshments." The duke flicked his chin in the direction of the food table. "Please seek her out. I am sure she wishes to see you again."

"Yes, of course, Your Grace." Rose felt the weight of another's glance. She turned, and her heart skipped frantically.

Colin, looking devastatingly handsome, bowed. His dark coat was paired with a golden vest and white cravat, and his dark waves were neatly styled. "Miss Grant."

"My Lord." She smiled, meeting his green-eyed gaze.

He greeted Amelia and then returned his attention to Rose. "Will you dance with me?"

"You waste little time, son," the duke said, grinning.

Rose bit her bottom lip to keep from smiling and accepted the marquess's hand.

* * *

COLIN'S HEART thudded in his chest with each spin and step

of the dance; he tried to steady it along with his nerves. Rose was undeniably the most beautiful woman in the room and equally superior when it came to matters of character. Was it possible he had won her affection?

They promenaded across the center of the room, and Colin caught the jealous glances of both men and women. The ladies, no doubt, had heard of Rose's residence at the gardener's cottage, and the men, clear from their intent stares, were captivated by Rose's beauty and grace.

He had hoped to wait until the ball was nearly over to speak with her, but the adrenaline rushing through his body urged him toward impatience.

The last chord of the song rang, and Rose curtsied from across the aisle. Her eyes were notably green. Had she been crying earlier? Or, was it only the light of candles playing tricks on him—perhaps even the blue of her dress causing the effect?

He took her hand, wrapping it around his arm. "Thank you. Will you walk outside with me?"

Rose's brows drew up, and the smallest line of worry appeared above her top lip. Colin leaned closer to hear her words amidst the crowd. "I would be delighted to, but... Lord Stratfordshire—people are staring. I worry you are drawing too much attention to yourself and me. If you wish to avoid gossip—"

"I do not care about gossip." He blinked, pulling her toward the terrace gardens. "I would rather speak to you than dance with the number of ladies that wish to ensnare me."

"My Lord." Rose leaned against his arm, slowing his pace, and Colin realized he had nearly dragged her to the terrace in his excitement. She laughed, and her eyes shone back at him with amusement. "What is so important that you must make me skip a step for each of yours?"

He laughed and set his free hand against a stone barrier to the gardens. Couples walked along the lit paths below, while others sat at benches. "That room, with all its greedy people, is suffocating and nearly intolerable. The dresses and polite speech, the bowing and curtsying, the introductions and flirtatious glances—I have already passed through formalities with you, and I prefer our conversation and company to any of that."

"Even the flirtatious glances?" Rose asked, pulling her hand from his arm.

He caught her gloved hand and pulled it to his chest. "Depending on where they originate."

Her eyes widened, and she stared at his hand over hers. "Then you mean to tease me."

"Not in the slightest." Suddenly, his planned speech felt as stiff as the room they had just left. Rose deserved more than that. "Will you walk with me in the gardens?"

"Yes, I would love to see these gardens, and that fountain…" Rose's lips spread into a large smile.

"My grandfather had the feature installed. The statue at the center of the fountain is of him, riding atop his stallion. My grandfather was the type that enjoyed such attention." Colin led her down the steps. He did not know where or how to begin. He only knew that the time had come to tell her how he felt. "Miss Grant, you look particularly pretty this evening."

"Thank you." They passed by the fountain and she stopped to get a better look at the statue. "I think you favor your mother's line, for I cannot see your likeness."

He nodded. "Thankfully."

"And why should you wish to look different from your grandfather?"

Colin's mouth went dry, and his voice cracked. "For the same reason you were happy to see your resemblance to your mother. Children naturally wish to resemble those they admire."

The water from the fountain trickled to the pool below, filling a momentary silence.

"I received your gift," Rose said, smiling up at him.

He had hoped Oliver would not mention the added pay or the order to take Rose and Amelia shopping. He blushed. "About that... I had hoped to remain anonymous."

She clasped her hands behind her back. Her eyes shimmered in the moonlight, and emotion seeped into her voice. "I figured, but a gift so lovely, with or without a card, deserves gratitude. Thank you. Your regard means very much to me."

Colin's stomach lodged in his throat. Rose was kind-hearted and pleasant but also undeniably guarded. She struggled to speak freely, to laugh unreservedly, to explain the past that troubled her so often. Though time had improved upon her, Rose continued to hold part of herself back.

But when she looked at him like that, all doubt fled. Her walls crumbled, and in place of them laid a simple truth; she cared for him. Perhaps as much as he cared for her. He placed his hand on her arm, guiding her toward a more private row of hedges.

"Rose." His head buzzed with the possibilities, but his heart clamored in a fit of nerves. "I had thought to wait to speak with you until after the ball, but I cannot. I think you well know my intentions. Since our first ride in the country, I recognized certain qualities in you—qualities that I admire. Though you are much too modest to admit it, I am sure you have heard how I searched for you. I sent letters to every possible connection, hoping they might know of your location. Some might have charged it to responsibility after your condition at the musicale, but that is not the full truth."

"No?" Rose's eyes glistened, and Colin noted the tears

balancing against the brim of her lower lashes. "Then why did you search for me?"

Colin placed a hand at her cheek. "I needed to find you, almost as much as I have grown to...to adore you. I cannot go a day without wishing to hear your voice, wishing to see your smile, wishing to hear your laughter."

Her breath grew shallow, and she pressed her forehead against his shoulder in what seemed to be an attempt to steady herself. "Nothing could make me happier than to hear you speak those words."

"There is so much more I wish to tell you, to ask you."

She lifted her chin and met his gaze. "Then do."

He brushed his other hand over a ringlet, tucking it behind her ear. His hand knocked against something metal. Prongs poked at his fingers, but he ignored them. "I have been hoping, no—praying, that you would wish to hear my question. Rose, I have to ask you..."

She turned, and the moonlight lit the side of her head, illuminating a golden comb decorated with rubies.

Colin stiffened. He studied the hairpiece, determined to detect discrepancies. However, as Rose turned toward the light, the moonlight struck it straight on, illuminating the etched outline of the orchard. His chest seemed to collapse against his heart, pressing until he gasped for breath.

"Rose, that comb..."

She laughed. "I simply adore it. When I first saw it, I knew it was intended for me—"

Colin pulled away in disbelief. *The musicale, Rose's tears, the duchess's refusal to speak of what happened*—everything blurred together. Was it possible Rose had taken it? He shook his head, not wanting to believe such a revolting idea. "Rose, I need you to answer honestly. Do you know what that comb signifies?"

Her brows knit together, and her cheeks grew darker. "If

you must hear it from my own lips, I will say it, but only to satisfy you." She swallowed and her gaze fell to the ground before she met his eyes again. "I imagine wearing this would be a sign that I'm to be…that this gift means you would wish me the future duchess of Andover…"

"No. No, Rose. You could not—you would not… it cannot be." Colin lifted his hands to his head, shaking back and forth. "You claim that comb as your own?"

She retreated from his touch, pulling the comb from her hair. The stolen symbol of his parents' union rested in her hands.

"What can you mean? You have given me every indication that you cared for me. You sent me this gift, and now, when I have come to your ball wearing it, you are… angry?" A broken sob tore from her lips.

"Lord Stratfordshire," called a servant a few feet away. "Your mother is asking for you. She requests a dance with her son."

Colin's head reeled. His mother, his ill and dear mother. He swallowed, lowering his glance to Rose's gloved hands. Nothing made sense—not the comb, not Rose's words, nor the ache in his chest that made breathing near impossible. How had he been so mistaken? How had he fallen into a trap? All this while, he had thought Rose different than her scheming aunt…but Rose had gone so far as to relocate herself onto his grounds! Rose, as beautiful and charming as she appeared, was no different than her sour apple of an aunt. With the sudden realization, came humiliation.

He plucked the comb from her hand. "Goodnight, Miss Grant. I am to dance with my mother, and you are free to return to the ballroom or to the cottage, but I should *not* wish to speak with you again."

CHAPTER 12

$\mathcal{T}$ears clouded Rose's vision. The darkness threatened to close in on her. She watched as the outline of the marquess disappeared up the stairs and into the ballroom.

She collapsed against a bench, allowing the tears to fall. In all her life, Rose had never felt more broken. Not the death of her mother, not the loss of the father she had never known, not even her aunt's attempt at suffocating Rose in a corset—nothing came close to the stabbing knives against her chest and throat.

The death of her parents had come as consequences of accidents and illnesses; Prudence's mistreatment stemmed from her narcissistic inability to look past jealousy and past misfortunes. But, Colin—Rose had allowed him in her heart. She cared for him, tried her best to allow herself to open up to him.

Her chest seemed to sever once more, and her heart crawled dangerously slow. Why had she allowed herself to hope for a future with the marquess? Why had she put her heart in the open? Oliver had been right. Colin would not offer for a lady staying with a servant.

A gentleman, a few feet away, whispered something to the lady on his arm, and they laughed.

Rose drew in five breaths, hardly bothering to exhale. She had been as contented as the couple before her only moments ago. Rose wiped a gloved finger beneath each eye and stood. She would not stay; Colin had been clear about his disgust in regard to her assumption.

She was a fool. Perhaps Prudence was right to lock her away. She marched to the ballroom and filed through the dancers, determined to find Amelia before she shed another tear. But with each step, her heart seemed to crack afresh. Colin was at the center of the room, dancing with the duchess.

His gaze met hers for a brief second, and his lips parted in surprise.

A thread of anger coursed through her, surprising her entirely. She was unaccustomed to the boiling in her stomach or the sharp words resting on the tip of her tongue. But how could she not feel something akin to anger? The marquess had strung her along, only to crush her in a vulnerable moment.

"Rose, what on earth?" Amelia asked, meeting Rose near the line of chairs. Amelia's lips lowered to a frown. "You look as if you've had a dreadful evening. Are you ill?"

Rose pressed a hand to her stomach and nodded. She did feel ill; that was no lie. "Please take me home."

Although appearing reluctant to leave the glittering ballroom, Amelia conceded and followed Rose to the row of carriages. They walked in silence, but tears began again once they were seated inside the dark conveyance.

The cottage was only a fifteen-minute ride from Stratfordshire, but each second seemed excruciatingly prolonged.

She released slow breaths and leaned against the window in an attempt to stifle conversation.

Aunt Amelia was an attentive aunt. She would have listened, perhaps even offered comfort. However, Rose could not bring herself to speak the words aloud—not yet. Colin did not want a future with Rose, and from his final words, she doubted he ever had.

She muffled a sob in her glove.

When they reached the cottage, Rose nearly sprinted from the carriage. She burst through the door, knocking into Oliver.

Her cousin caught her by the shoulders, surveying her tears and listening to her broken sobs. "Rose?"

She collapsed against him, crying into his chest. "I thought…Oh, Oliver. I was terribly mistaken. I thought Lord Stratfordshire cared for me, and I said as much, but now he does not wish to speak to me ever again."

Oliver sighed, brushing a hand through her curls. "Oh, Rose."

Amelia entered the home and placed a hand against Rose's back. "I knew it was more than illness that had her wishing to leave. Rose, did Lord Stratfordshire truly refuse to offer for you after that gift of the golden comb?"

Rose's cries were answer enough, and she gasped for breath amidst her weeping. She could almost hear the sound of Prudence scolding her. *You were foolish to think he cared for you, child. You were naïve and silly. You deserve every bit of your humiliation.*

"Rose, I am so sorry." Oliver pulled her to the sofa. "You must rest. Mother, get her tea."

She sunk into the sofa, feeling as helpless as an infant child. Why could she not get a grip on her emotions? Why wouldn't the tears stop?

Oliver set a pillow under her head and wrapped a blanket

over her trembling shoulders. "Perhaps news from home will do the trick? I saw this letter on the hall table from this morning. Did you not see it? It is from your friend, Mr. Paul Garvey. Shall I read it to you?"

Rose numbly shook her head, though she doubted a single word would hold any meaning.

"Right," Oliver said, shuffling to retrieve the letter. He opened it in haste and returned to Rose's side. *"Dear Rose, I thank you for your previous letter. I am glad to hear you are well, and I hope my next news will not cause you too much distress. I did as you said and paid a visit to your grandfather while your aunt was out. Only, she returned before I had left, intercepting the letter—"*

Rose shot up. She tore the paper from Oliver's hands, scanning the words for affirmation of the sinking feeling in her stomach.

Dear Rose,

I thank you for your previous letter. I am glad to hear you are well, and I hope my next news will not cause you too much distress. I did as you said and paid a visit to your grandfather while your aunt was out, two days ago. Only, your aunt returned before I had left, intercepting the letter I took to read to him, and, consequently, she has learned of your whereabouts.

Rose, Prudence has gone mad. I neglected to tell you the extent in my last letter, but your departure has seemed to ignite an even more vile woman. She spit upon me and sent me away. I am quite sure she is set upon your undoing, though I do not pretend to understand her method.

Since that fateful day, my father has heard gossip of some attempt to bring you out of favor with the duke and his family. And just now, as I write this letter, my father tells me of a package that you must not open.

Rose, after the incident at the musicale, I fear for your safety.

Please, take care, and send me word as soon as you are able. Tell me I am not too late.

Paul

Rose fell back to the sofa. Her tears turned to disbelief. "You say this letter arrived earlier today? Why didn't anyone give it to me?"

Oliver shrugged. "You were preoccupied with preparations for the duke's ball. I set it on the hall table, thinking you would retrieve it in a moment of convenience."

Rose buried her face in the pillow. When she had seen the comb, with its apple tree and rubies, she was sure Colin had it made for her. Clearly, Prudence had planted the comb, but why? How could a comb alter Colin's affection? And how could she ask him now, when he never wished to speak to her again?

* * *

COLIN ADJUSTED the papers on the desk in front of him. He squinted, trying to make out the figures of his secretary's penmanship. Goodness, why was the room so dark and hot? He rose to the window and pulled back the drapes.

He leaned against the window frame for a moment. His head pounded from the ball's festivities and, more surely, his dismissal of Rose. He still did not understand how she had gotten the comb or why she had been so brazen to wear it. Her behavior went against everything he had come to know and love about her.

Or, what he *thought* he knew and loved about her.

He pushed open the window, and the cool morning air blew in, catching his papers on the desk and carrying them in a spiral across the room, scattering in every direction. He darted in an attempt to catch them, cursing all the while.

"Colin!" The duchess stood across the study. She scowled.

"Control your tongue, won't you? I have not seen you lose your temper like this since you were a child."

"Mother." Colin's cheeks darkened in shame. He was not one to curse, nor to lose his temper often. He stood, with an armful of papers, and faced her. "Good morning, I did not hear you come in."

She lifted a hand to her hip and tilted her head. Dark bags hung beneath each eye, wrinkling as she coughed into her shoulder. "How could you? With all that rattling of papers and obscenities, I am surprised you are here at all. How unlike you."

"Yes, but then the investments father has charged me with are far outside my realm of comfort." Colin's shoulders fell forward, and he set about sorting the papers at the desk. He could not look at her; he was never skilled at hiding his emotions and thoughts from the duchess.

She said nothing in return, but Colin felt her critical eye from where she stood.

The duchess had inquired about Rose multiple times throughout the ball, wondering when she might have the honor of meeting her again or if Colin would ask her to dance a second set. He had done his best to avoid her questions, and thankfully, there were more than enough partners and acquaintances that battled for his attention.

"How long will you make me wait?"

Colin's chin snapped higher. "Wait? For what?"

His attempt was futile. She crossed her arms, and a look of sadness lit her features. "I know you better than you like to admit. Before the ball, your face beamed with excitement. You could hardly stop smiling. In fact, your entire attitude gave me the impression you wished to offer for Miss Grant. You said as much too."

Colin shook his head. "Beamed with excitement? I doubt that."

Her silence grew thick, and she waited for a long moment to speak. "And then you changed, only half an hour into the ball. Do not mistake me. You were quite dutiful in your attentions to our guests, you danced, and you were as charming as any lady might hope for. But, I could see your mind had wandered far away, as did your heart. You may have been present last night, but that was only a technicality. You were somewhere else entirely."

The duchess knew what so many did not; if one wished to draw a subject out, astute observations were much more effective than questions. Colin's throat grew scratchy, and he swallowed hard. "I will not deny what you say. Miss Grant, it seems—she is not what I thought, what I hoped."

"Oh?" The duchess strode across the room and rested her hands on his desk. "And what have you discovered?"

He dropped his head into his heads. He hardly knew what Rose was or was not. His thoughts circumnavigated his head like a horse track, competing with one another in a hopeless struggle.

"Colin?"

He opened his top drawer and tossed the comb against the desktop.

The duchess gasped. "Where did you find this?"

His shoulders quaked, and his eyes pooled. "Rose wore it last night." He paused, drawing in a breath. "When I spotted it, I tried to ask her about it, but her answers only furthered my conclusion. I believe she stole it from you the night of the musicale. I believe she sought me out purposely in an attempt to gain my affection and title."

The duchess picked up the comb, inspecting every detail. Her brows drew together, and she chewed on the inside of her cheek.

"Well? Can you blame me for turning away from her? Can you blame me for my melancholy mood? I have lost what I supposed to be the only woman I might love." Colin's voice cracked, and he cupped his hands to his cheeks once more.

"I do not blame you, not at all. You have been the object of many women's attempts at status and fortune. Trusting is difficult, even for a man as good as you."

He lifted a brow. "You think I am wrong? Mother, how else can you explain her having the comb? She had the nerve to claim I gifted it to her."

The duchess clasped the comb to her chest and sighed. "I have not told you what happened on the night of the musicale for two reasons—to protect Miss Grant's privacy and to investigate the events. However, if you are ready to reject the affection of such a dear girl, I feel I must inform you. Her aunt nearly took Miss Grant's life that night."

Colin's head jerked backward. He rubbed at his eyes. His mind flashed to the day at the orchard when he caught Rose in a moment of contemplation. *"I left under difficult circumstances," she had said.* Colin swallowed again. "How so?"

The duchess moved to his side of the desk and placed her hands on his shoulders. "Prudence always had her ways —she was the master of disguising her scandalous attempts. She was no different with her niece. She used a trick-corset, one made for short periods of wear, to nearly suffocate Miss Grant. I will spare you the details, but I have had the garment examined, and my lawyers tell me there is reason enough to charge Prudence with assault. Did you not notice Prudence's indifference to Rose's suffering on the night of the musicale, the way she dismissed her niece so callously?"

Colin winced.

"Let me assure you—Prudence could not have been more unfeeling. Now, I must tell you something more. My comb was quite intact when Miss Grant left. I took it out after the second set of songs, for my head did ache with worry for

Miss Grant. I placed it in my reticule, but by the time we left, it was gone."

"Then you…" His stomach sunk to his knees. The things he had said to Rose, the way he had looked at her… Colin rose from the chair and walked to the open window. The breeze did little to calm the tightness in his chest or the regret lodging into the back of his throat. "You mean to say that Rose did not take the comb, and you are sure of it?"

"Yes."

The word stabbed at him. Tears slipped down his cheeks, and he took a shaky breath. How could he have doubted Rose? How could he have left her without a moment to explain? He trembled against the frame of the window, catching a glimmer of his reflection in the glass.

He turned away; he had never been more disgusted with the image glaring back at him.

CHAPTER 13

*D*ear Niece,

    After much distress, I have learned your where-abouts. Tell me, did you intend to go on living there forever without sending me a single word? You must know what trouble you caused. My head has throbbed from worry, and my joints have turned stiff. Have you forgotten all my efforts to procure you a future? Are you so ungrateful?

    In other news, I think you would be happy to hear that I received a visit from Mr. Higgins last week. He has offered for your hand, despite your leaving (and the scandal it has presented to those that know).

    I shall come to Andover myself to collect you in a day. I urge you to consider Mr. Higgins, for after your taking residence in a servant's cottage, I am quite sure no man of standing would wish to offer for your hand.

    Prudence

* * *

THERE ARE moments when words fall short—Rose had

learned that long ago, when her mother had died, and a disapproving aunt had assumed the role of her guardian. Now, Oliver and Amelia continued to inquire after her well-being, but Rose lacked answers.

Nearly three days had passed since the ball. Rose felt no closer to understanding what had happened. The world made as little sense as a spinning kaleidoscope; her own aunt was determined to ruin her, Colin had forsaken her at the sight of a comb, and she had nowhere to go but felt unable to remain near Stratfordshire.

She walked the Orchards; they seemed the only place left with order and peace. The harvest had come early, and Oliver had ordered additional gardeners for the picking of apples. Rose set out to volunteer, eager to busy her hands.

"Rose, you have come." Oliver carried a pile of stacked baskets. He set them on the grass and lifted his hat. "Have you worked a day in an orchard before?"

Rose smiled, but the effort was forced, empty. She pulled her straw bonnet on, tying the ribbon beneath her chin. "Not once."

Her cousin laughed. "The task is simple enough. Take the apple and twist upward. Do not pull the apple downward—that can damage the branches."

"Sounds simple enough." She took a basket. "Any other commands, Head Gardener?"

"Yes." Oliver put his arm on Rose's shoulder. "Do try to enjoy yourself, and take care on the step ladder."

"As you wish."

Rose wandered the rows of apples until she settled on a silent row near the southeast edge of the plot. The views across the duke's land were lovely, yet she was still surrounded by the straight aisles of beautiful fruit. The trees reached about ten feet high, and the bright blue sky loomed overhead.

The beauty of the day contrasted drastically with her despondent heart. Sadness had become her inevitable companion. Yet, with the sun shining against the trees, the rushing of wind against her cheek, and the occasional songs of the birds, Rose could not help but feel lighter.

Her future could not be so desperate as to warrant returning to Prudence or accepting Mr. Higgins. Marrying Mr. Higgins was a cowardly escape. She did not love him and did not think herself capable. He was more than twice her age.

Perhaps Rose only needed more sunlight and time. Perhaps there was still hope coloring her future. Her baskets filled quickly, and she made a game of discovering the hidden gems, the ones that were just right for picking—firm, crisp, ruby-red colored apples.

Rose gasped. A memory, one she had forgotten until now, came with such force that Rose nearly fell from her step ladder.

Her mother leaned over the counter beside Mrs. Blackburn, studying the recipe in front of them.

"What shall I add next?" Rose stood at her mother's side, hanging on Lillian's floral-patterned apron. "Shall I get the rolling pin, Mama?"

Her mother laughed, and the sound was magic—warm, tender, but equally amused. "We have apples to wash and slice, darling. The filling must be finished before the crust."

Rose clutched the branches to steady herself, for with the flashes of faces and smells came sounds. *Her mother's laughter.* Rose closed her eyes and leaned against the trunk of the tree. If only Rose could replay that sound over and over in her ears, she would do so until she grew dizzy with joy.

The memory was so simple; there was nothing spectacular about it—in terms of significance or impact. Yet, Rose could not bite back the smile and the unexpected tears blurring her vision.

Lillian Grant had chosen joy over anything else. Wishing for a child for almost nine years, becoming a widow once pregnant, and caring for a blind father-in-law—Rose's mother had not been dealt ease. Not to mention a sister-in-law that seethed with jealousy...

Yet, Rose's mother had chosen joy.

Prudence had poisoned Colin's opinion of Rose. Just the thought caused her posture to stiffen and she teetered once more. How could Rose choose joy? How could she forgive Colin for his distrust and her subsequent heartbreak? How could she forgive *herself* for believing the marquess would offer for her?

Where was Rose's mother to teach her? Recollections acted as a poor substitute.

She climbed down from the ladder and set the basket in the shade. She sprinted across the row of apple trees, stopping only when she reached the brick wall surrounding the orchard. Running was a temporary fix to pain, but the need to counter her ache had propelled her. She leaned against the wall, struggling to catch her breath. Would her heart ever heal from Colin's rejection? Did love like that ever leave?

"Miss Grant."

She jumped at the sound. She knew that voice almost as much as her own. "Lord Stratfordshire," she said, not daring to meet his glance. "Do you make it a habit of startling young ladies?" Her voice trembled, and her attempt at lightheartedness was weak.

Colin stood only yards away, wearing his riding boots. His horse trailed behind him, feeding on the grass. Colin shifted his weight. "I suppose I have."

Rose turned from him, gazing across the fields around

the orchard. "You told me that you wished to never speak to me again."

"Yes, but I was wrong to do so."

She winced, and her heart rose to her throat, beating wildly until she could scarcely breathe.

"Rose, I once compared you to a sunflower. Do you remember?"

Rose nodded.

"You have the fairest heart of anyone I have ever met, and I cannot believe how I behaved. I can only say that my shock at seeing something my mother treasures, in your hands..." Colin shuffled closer, and his boots crunched a patch of dry grass. "I'm not attempting to win you over with excuses. I am asking—no, begging. If you saw any good in me before, will you try to once more? I have made a horrible mistake. I just came from speaking with my mother. She told me about Prudence and the musicale..."

Rose released a cracked sob, quickly covering her mouth.

Colin continued, "That comb—I only knew it had been stolen from my mother the night of the musicale. I mistook your words the night of the ball, and I have made a wretched mess of things. I cannot rationalize my actions, but I can explain why I acted the way I did and said the things I said. Will you allow me to try?"

Her shoulders shook. She longed to hear his words, but her broken and angered heart still felt the deep wounds of betrayal. Humiliation, confusion, sadness—could words patch such brokenness?

Colin stepped in front of her, lifting her chin. "Rose, please." His storm-colored eyes looked every bit as troubled as the sea. Emotion gleamed back at her, and his lips pressed into a frown. "Please?"

Compassion clawed at the back of her throat, and her anger softened. "You may try."

He inhaled sharply. "Your aunt wishes to tear us apart, by any means necessary. She nearly suffocated you, and she played upon my greatest fear—being tricked into loving a woman more interested in my title than my heart."

The heaviness in her heart lifted.

"That comb belongs to my mother, given to her by my father on their wedding. He proposed in the orchard, you see. It disappeared the night of the musicale. When I saw you wearing it and you said you knew it was intended for you, I mistakenly pieced things together. I am a fool for thinking you capable of such scheming. I am ashamed."

Rose released a slow breath. "I was also a fool to think I was free of Prudence. Her jealousy extends far, and she punishes me for every injustice she has received. I should not have ever accepted a gift without tag. I only thought it was you because…" Her eyes clamped shut. "The apple tree etchings and rubies."

His hands cupped each side of her cheeks.

She blinked back tears. His touch was warm and gentle, and she did not wish her pride to keep her from him. Happiness was worth more than anger and misplaced justice. "Do you think you could love me after what has passed between us?"

His lips parted, and a puff of air escaped, brushing against her cheek. "Do I think…?" He shook his head, and laughter mixed with his tears. "Rose, I adore you. I have spent the last hours, and night, in a fearful state. After not even allowing you a chance to explain, I worried I had lost you forever. I love you wholly, and I will continue loving you until my last breath. Please, say you will marry me?"

Heat burned in her chest, radiating to her fingertips and toes. Forgiveness no longer seemed a question—instead a passing ship along shining waters. Her breath shook in relief.

"Please?" he asked, sniffling and smiling all at one. "I cannot imagine a more beautiful soul to spend forever with."

Rose placed a hand against his cheek, staring back at him. Happiness muffled her answer to an almost inaudible "yes".

And then his lips met hers—urgently and unabashedly thorough. With each movement, he drew away a piece of her doubt, a portion of the poison that Prudence had placed between them.

Colin pulled her closer, lifting her into his arms and spinning her around.

She laughed, and the sudden realization struck her—she carried more than her mother's resemblance. She carried Lillian's laugh too. Her heart swelled. Such happiness had not seemed possible moments before. Yet, there she was—spinning in the arms of her future husband, with a future as bright as the afternoon sun. Like her mother, Rose would choose joy.

* * *

ROSE PEEKED from the edge of the parlor window.

The carriage swayed against the broken path, stopping with a jolt. The door opened, and Prudence stepped onto the walk. Her nose pinched, and she paused to scowl at the sight of the cottage.

"Are you ready to face her?" Colin whispered in her ear, clutching her hand.

"Undoubtedly."

Prudence knocked with the force of a hammer, repeating the gesture when Rose did not answer straight away. "It is Prudence, Rose. Open this door immediately."

Rose swallowed hard. After much thought, she pitied her aunt; Prudence was bound to be even unhappier than she already was. "Coming," she called, lifting the latch.

"Gracious, child. Did you not receive my letter? I have come to collect you. Mr. Higgins has been as patient as can be hoped for, considering the circumstances, and you—"

"Why did you send the comb?" Rose folded her arms.

"Send the—what nonsense are you speaking? Now, collect your belongings and come." Prudence wafted a hand in front of her. "How have you abided this place? It smells of smoke and sweat and filthy young men."

Rose smiled. "My cousins are home, Aunt. Please lower your voice."

"And why should I? I would have thought you happy to receive my letter and return home after the disasters you've encountered at both the musicale and the ball."

Rose nodded. "All thanks to you."

"Well, course I couldn't allow you to make a complete fool of yourself—I – "

Colin stepped from the parlor, meeting Prudence. He towered over her. "Mrs. Grant, we meet again."

"Lord Stratfordshire... you..." Her mouth fell open. "What do I owe this pleasure? Have you come to chastise my niece as I have? I heard she was spotted wearing the very comb the duchess lost that fateful night—"

"Not another word, Mrs. Grant. I have decided to show you compassion, if only because of your kindhearted niece."

Prudence almost lost her balance. "Pardon?"

"I have asked for Rose's hand in marriage, Mrs. Grant." Colin wrapped his arm around Rose's back. His eyes seemed to brighten. "And so, I have found a lovely home in Bath for you. Rose and I will settle at Grant Estate and care for Lord Grant after the wedding, and you—you will stay far away."

Prudence gasped. Her cheeks flamed red, and her eyes bulged. "And why on earth would I agree to such absurd terms?"

Colin's eyes narrowed. "You will agree to such conditions

in exchange for my silence. After your schemes—the corset and the comb—I have plenty of proof to send you away to the stocks, Mrs. Grant. Or, perhaps even worse, enough ammunition to ruin your reputation once again. So, what will it be?"

"You know," Prudence said, clenching her teeth. "I hear Bath is lovely this time of year. Besides, I rather do detest sharing my home."

She turned on her heel, returning to the carriage almost as quickly as she came. With her angry shriek, the driver snapped his whip and the carriage bounced inside a cloud of dust.

Rose leaned against Colin's chest and released the breath she had been holding. Prudence was gone, with all her disapproval, scoldings, punishments, and gloom. And now Rose was encompassed in safety, peace, and unimaginable joy. The contrast nearly stole her breath all over again.

"Well," Colin said, cracking a smile. "I suppose that could have gone worse."

He led her out the door toward the gardens.

"Indeed." Rose moved to her toes, planting a kiss against his cheek. "Thank you. I do not think I could have been the one to bear the news. Despite all her horridness, I do not wish her unhappy."

Colin's eyes widened, and he leaned closer. "Rose, with you at my side, I might make a decent man after all."

He pulled her into an embrace, kissing her softly but thoroughly once again.

Her heart thudded, and happiness threatened to overwhelm her. All the days and adventures she'd shared with Colin spun through her thoughts. She had finally found her home, and no amount of poisonous dealings would ever taint her happiness again.

. . .

The End

If you enjoyed this story, **please leave a review on Amazon.**

For a complete list of Heather Chapman's books or to sign up for her newsletter, visit http://www.heatherchapmanauthor.com

The Fairest Heart is a stand-alone sweet regency romance novella, part of the Once Upon a Regency Series. Make sure to read the other books in the series:

The Midnight Heiress by Ashtyn Newbold (Coming March 2019)

Spun of Gold by Jen Geigle Johnson (Coming April 2019)

Beauty's Rose by Rebecca J. Greenwood (Coming May 2019)

Proving Miss Price by Jessilyn Stewart Peaslee (Coming June 2019)

ABOUT THE AUTHOR

Being the youngest of four sisters and one very tolerant older brother, Heather grew up on a steady diet of chocolate, Jane Austen, Anne of Green Gables, Audrey Hepburn, and the other staples of female moviedom and literature. These stories, along with good teachers, encouraged Heather throughout high school and college to read many of the classics in literature, and later, to begin writing her own stories of romance and adventure. After meeting and marrying her husband Mark, Heather graduated magna cum laude from Brigham Young University and settled down in a small farming community in southeastern Idaho with her husband and four children. In her spare time, Heather enjoys time spent with family, volleyball, piano, the outdoors, and almost anything creative. She is the author of *The Second Season*, *The Forgotten Girl*, and *Forever Elle*. You can find out more about Heather and her writing by visiting the website heatherchapmanauthor.com.

Made in the USA
San Bernardino, CA
20 July 2019